Against the Hidden River

Against the Hidden River

Michael W. Cox

MAMMOTH books
DuBois, Pennsylvania

First edition

ISBN: 978-1-59539-035-6
MAMMOTH books
is an imprint of
MAMMOTH press inc.
7 Juniata Street
DuBois, Pennsylvania 15801

www.mammothbooks.org

Cover photo by author
Author photo by Jon Ritz
Cover design & page layout by Jason Enterline

Production by Offset Paperback Manufacturers, Inc.

ACKNOWLEDGMENTS

Publication credits for these stories, some of which appeared in earlier form, are as follows: "Send Off" in *South Asian Review*; "Oak Park, Illinois" in *Columbia;* "Old School" and "Away from Home" in *Florida English*; "Island" (as "Three Rivers") in *West Branch*; "The It Boy" in *Passages North* (reprinted in *Tartts 3*); "Unfinished Business" in *Aethlon*; "My Mother's Lovers" in *Cimarron Review*; "Grove" in *ACM*; "One Dark Sky" in *Salt Hill*; and "Leopold and Loeb" in *Florida Review*.

I am grateful to the editors of each of these venues—in particular Vijay Chauhan, Kate Hanson, Barry Silesky, Stephanie Carpenter, and Russ Kesler —and to good friends who have read my drafts down through the years: Cathy Cox, Dick Strojan, Jon Ritz, and Alessandra Lynch.

CONTENTS

"Chi siete voi che contro al cieco fiume
fuggita avete la pregione etterna?"

("Who are you —who, against the hidden river,
were able to escape the eternal prison?")

—Dante Alighieri, *Purgatorio* I.40-41

SEND OFF

My last night in Chicago, full moon in the sky, my bedroom window a vivid gray, Nielsen brought home a whore. He wasn't supposed to be home at all, had said he'd give me wide berth, let me finish packing my things and leave. But there he was at the door, talking through the inch of space the chain allowed.

"Sunil," he whispered.

I had heard the scratching, the chain catching.

"Suuuniiiil!" louder, sounding like Marley's Ghost.

Habit carried me to the door. I pulled tight my robe and undid the chain and Nielsen stepped inside, grinning like a drunk. He was not a tall man, and I looked down to see that his hair, which he grew long on the side to cover his crown, had shifted, our hallway light glimmering off globules of sweat. I had spent six years keeping Nielsen out of sight of my parents when they visited from back east. His love of alcohol and fast (and cheap) women would have caused my mother, born and raised in India, to reach for her Nexium. My father, also Indian and a gastroenterologist (weak stomachs ran in the family, and my father had decided long ago to make them a subject of study), would have lectured me, as they love to say in small-town Pennsylvania, till the cows come home. They knew little about Nielsen except that, given his surname, he wasn't an Indian. "I hope he's a nice boy," my mother said, and said again (and again), at any mention of his name.

The prostitute stepped in behind him. She was very pretty, in a made up, short-skirted sort of way. A little higher class than Nielsen's usual. And she had a good eye, drunk as she was:

"You were right," she slurred. "He really is a cutie."

"Told you," Nielsen said. "Tall, dark, and brutally handsome." He winked at me. "You want to have a drink with us?"

"Why?" I asked, still half—no, three quarters—asleep.

The woman suddenly kissed me, not afraid to use her tongue—the kind of move you don't forget for a good twenty years. "Whoa," I said. I stepped back and fell over one of my boxes, landed on another. Something broke inside—something that crunched when I shifted.

Nielsen pulled me to my feet, my robe bunched in his fists. "I'll take care of that," he said. "Don't you worry." Sweat dripped into his eye and he blinked. "Rosalyn," he shouted over his shoulder. "Hey, Rosalyn, do the thing."

Rosalyn smiled and posed provocatively, chest protruding, hands sliding along her hips. Nielsen was mesmerized, and with good reason—not only did Rosalyn have a pretty face, she had a figure to match, and she liked to put on a show and do a little bump and grind, dancing sinuously between my packed boxes and stepping onto our coffee table—a cube, really, an actual butcher's block where my parents' cups of tea had sat only a few weeks before. I tried not to imagine my mother's face, were she to witness this scene, a half-naked half-African woman making a come-hither face, replete with slippery tongue, for her only son's bemused eyes.

My parents' semi-annual visits to Chicago had launched two cleaning marathons (and evidence-hiding sessions) a year, one in September, a few weeks before school began, and one in late March, at Spring Break. "I was so much happier when you were at Bucknell," my mother, glancing around my dimly-lit Chicago apartment, had said one spring of my undergraduate years. At Bucknell, just a three-hour drive from home, my parents could (and did) drop in completely unannounced. None of their visits were occasions for embarrassment, but I credit that at least partly to luck—that, and better decision-making at the time concerning just who it was I chose for a roommate.

The current one slid to his knees before the altar of our butcher's block, raising his arms to snap his fingers to a beat only he and Rosalyn could register. "Dance, baby," Nielsen moaned. And dance Rosalyn did, grinding it out until suddenly she rubbed her nose, violently, and sneezed. "Oh my god," she said. "You have a cat." She sneezed again, a sneeze that would shame a fireman. She dug through her purse—for an antihistamine or a Kleenex, presumably. "I fucking hate cats," Rosalyn said, blowing her nose. "I mean, they're pretty to look at, but all that fur!" She blew again, and Nielsen wiped crazily at his face.

The slight possibility that Nielsen might one day be a colleague of mine (or worse, my chair) flashed through my mind; otherwise, I might have taken the opportunity to tell him how much I'd grown to hate being his roommate. This wasn't the last straw—there was never a last straw, that wasn't my style, more Indian, I suppose, than American. But I had had enough. "Nielsen, old friend," I began—they both looked at me, Rosalyn sniffling, Nielsen still wiping—"thanks for the offer of a drink, something I rarely, if ever, have, but truly, I have to get some rest. Big day tomorrow, as you know." I looked at Rosalyn. "No offense," I said. "I mean, seriously, you're stunning, as these things go."

And she was stunning, objectively speaking, but she looked hurt, which seemed strange (she was no snarler, like Nielsen's usual tart punk). Nielsen—just as hurt, apparently—made a face, lower lip protruding baby style. I shook my head and walked into my room, closed my door and threw my latch. He called my name once, with gusto, and then a second time, flat. And then I heard them talking, and then, shortly after, Nielsen's bedroom door closing with a thud.

Nielsen was a special case. He'd been working on his dissertation in ethnography for a shaky five years. Something to do with dialectic culture in Chicago's South Side. I couldn't really say what it was about beyond that, because Nielsen, as much as he liked to talk, had given me only the vaguest outline. The project had the usual grad student baggage: Too much theory, not enough application. But I knew Nielsen's M.O., or as he called it, his "method": In the morning, he'd take Rosalyn to a nice restaurant and play twenty questions: What neighborhood did you grow up in? What color was your father? Your mother? What schools did you attend? Mind blurry with alcohol, he'd scribble short-hand on his napkin while his "research subject" chattered away.

I lay down and tried not to listen to them in the next room, needing my sleep for the 10-hour drive I had planned for that day. My cat—a gift from my mother—sat at the end of the bed looking at me. She hated these late-night interruptions, but with Nielsen in the house, she (like me) had learned to live with them. She got up, kneaded the blanket and repositioned herself in exactly the same spot as before. As I was dropping off I heard footsteps in the apartment above me. Jacintha. We had awakened her, late, yet again. I had been with her only hours before, she dressed in a lavender sari, I in a summer jacket and nice shoes—rare for me, very rare for her. The sari was the kind of thing she wore to please her parents, usually, though it had pleased me, too, to see it.

"Do you like me in this," she had asked, "all traditional?" She turned for me, raising her arms and tilting her body in what I can only describe as an elegant dipping bow from Indian classical dance.

"Very much," I had said, and we laughed. I took this image with me to my dreams.

In the morning, I found Rosalyn passed out on the toilet, a lit cigarette dangling from her lips, the bathroom door wide. I gently squeezed the cigarette and pulled it from her lips, laid it on the sink beneath the spigot, which dripped. The cigarette hissed. On my way out the door I saw Nielsen sprawled across his water bed, face down, like a corpse in a pool.

Ah, Nielsen. To think that one day you'll clean up your act, become a responsible man and go on to marry one of your Rosalyns. You wouldn't be the first, you of the divorced parents, the alcoholic mother, the cheating father, the pot and drugs and broken windows of your youth. What choice did you have but to wander through this maze? And what choice did I have, but to stand back like an alien and marvel at your passage?

I walked to McDonald's and made use of their plumbing. A father had just finished changing his baby girl at the sink. He looked at me, laughed, said I looked as tired as he felt. "Thanks," I said. At the counter I ordered a small cup of coffee. I drank it there, staring at the park across the street. City ball was being played, kids in uniforms, boys leaping across the court and jamming balls, blocking shots, and generally flying—all this at 8:30 a.m. It made me tired just to watch them. I got a second cup of coffee and thought about my new life ahead. I had a full-time position lined up at a small college in the center of Florida, just south of Orlando (where, my mother informed me, a small but potent Indian community was building. "Go there immediately when you arrive," she insisted. "Join a club. The Mathurs, old friends, are there"). I was tired of student life, roommates, late nights and cheap eats. Not that I planned to live like a sultan or even a prince. But I needed a change, even if some of those I was leaving behind I would be sad not to see. I thought of Jacintha, our evening before, the lake, the breeze, her beautiful smile. She cared about me in a way no one else did, but it had taken me too long to figure that out. I had never quite mastered the art of juggling career aspirations with family building, and had resisted my mother's every attempt to meet Jacintha, imagining the relentless thrust of every conversation thereafter. I needed Jacintha to mean something just for me, something my parents couldn't touch.

When I got back home, Nielsen and Rosalyn were gone. The cat was hungry, and I fed her her last meal in the city of Chicago. I opened the box of plates. Only one had been broken; the one just beneath it was a little scratched, but you could see the scratches only if you held the plate to the window, for natural light. I loved those plates, one of the few indulgences I had allowed myself as a graduate student. I finished packing my toiletries, another box filled with important papers and my work in progress. I pushed my mattress against the wall and swept my room. The cat watched me from the window sill. Then she looked outside, her tail atwitch.

Tuttle came by at 10:00. Nearly silent, focused on the task at hand, he helped me load the mattress, the boxes, and the spare bits of furniture. I gave my cat the tranquilizer and put her in her travel-case and took her down to the truck, cracking the windows just an inch—I had parked it out of the sunlight anyway, so the cab would not heat up. I pulled the truck's cargo door shut and put a master-lock on it. I went inside, wrote Nielsen a check for some money he'd spotted me for my last month's rent, deducting five dollars for the plate and leaving the pieces on the butcher's block beside the check. I put a stickie beside the pieces and wrote "last night!" on it. I slipped the edge of the check under the stickie, pulled shut the apartment door, locked it, and slid the key under the door. I was free.

"How does it feel?" Tuttle, standing beside his car, asked drily when I got to the street.

I looked at him, then I looked back at my old window. "Disembodied," I said.

"You're just hungry," Tuttle said. "Or maybe I'm projecting." Tuttle was in a foul mood, one he never recognized but one all his friends knew—lack of a woman, his acquaintances, shallow to the end, would say. We got in his car and he drove us to I-HOP. The parking lot was full.

"Try 52nd," I said.

"I know what to try, Sunil," Tuttle snapped, taking a side street off the parking lot and rolling onto 52nd. He drove slowly and we both scoped the street.

"There's a place," I said.

"Where?"

"Up there, where that big black guy is double-parked."

The man was standing in the street, talking to someone on the sidewalk. Tuttle zipped into the empty spot, which the big black guy, apparently, had been planning to fill. "Get out of there!" he shouted, looking murderously at Tuttle.

We sat there a little shocked.

"That's totally rude," Tuttle said.

"He must've been planning to back in," I said.

"You heard me, cockroach," the man said, pointing at Tuttle. "Get out," throwing his thumb.

The man was huge. A seven-footer, maybe even a professional ball player, a back-up or recent call-up. I thought maybe I had seen him on ESPN, and I rarely watched TV. He got inside his car and started to back it up, slamming on his brakes for effect. Then he scooted forward a foot, maybe, giving us a touch of room in which to maneuver. The Benz just sat there, its back-up lights brightly lit.

"I think you should do like he says," I said.

"Huh uh," Tuttle said.

Usually I liked Tuttle much more than Nielsen. During my early years in Chicago he'd been a stable friend and colleague, making progress though our degree program on a pace with me. But then his marriage went sour, and he entered a darker phase. "I'm tired of assholes," he said. "Especially big assholes who throw their weight around." I had seen him like this before; something happened in that blond head of his. He'd jumped off a boat one day in Lake Michigan, no warning, leaving me to figure out the ropes of his sail boat, literally, so I could pull it back round to pick him up from the drink. He'd taken a pool stick to an opponent one night in a bar, using the tip to blue his prey's clean white shirt again and again with strong harsh taps. And on this occasion, the Benz before him, Tuttle managed skillfully to swing his ancient Buick out and dip sharply right, sideswiping the man's Benz. The big black man went walleyed as we slid by, scraping off his paint and chrome.

"You hit his car," I said, as Tuttle took a right turn onto Harper.

"No shit," Tuttle said.

Tuttle waited patiently for the red light to change at 51st, where traffic was thick. He seemed calmer, more relaxed, as if his spot of violence had done him good. I, on the other hand, looked in the side mirror, waiting for the man to pull his Benz around the corner and come after us. Tuttle took out a stick of gum, folded it, and touched it to his tongue. My head, meanwhile, was clangorous with my father's voice, berating me for my inability to choose the right friends. Back in PA my parents had done a lot of vetting, choosing my Little League team, the school that I attended, and nearly all my friends, each of whom had been required, more or less subtly, to appear before them and be quizzed about what their parents did, where they lived, etc. (the kind of thing I one day realized that Nielsen, my roommate, was an eerie echo of, given his dissertation's "methodology"—maybe it was subliminal familiarity that had led me to choose him in the first place). Such vetting didn't matter so much back in Somerset, where everyone knew everyone else and we were one of five Indian families in the whole county (3 doctors, 2 electrical engineers, 5 stay-at-home-moms, 17 Indian-American children). It got a little harder for them when I went off to college, and by grad school I had more or less conceived of the perfect plan: to attend a school in a community where my parents somehow miraculously knew no Indian, regardless of how many Indians the school employed. After thorough and surreptitious research, I realized that Chicago and Hyde Park fit the bill, perfectly.

The light finally turned and Tuttle took a right and then another and pulled instantly into a suddenly freed-up spot in front of I-HOP. "Whoa, check it out," he said, gesturing at his luck. I could see 52nd Street clearly from where we sat. I could see the Benz owner standing beside his car, running his finger along the crease Tuttle's Buick had just made.

Tuttle got out. "Come on," he said. "I'm hungry."

I got out. "You want to eat now? He's right there," I said, nodding. "All he has to do is look this way."

"Screw him," Tuttle said, and started for the door.

Tuttle was 5'10", if that. Maybe a hundred and forty pounds of stubborn white meat. Like me, he had been a graduate student in sociology at the University of Chicago, and like me, he had a job lined up for the fall, so I couldn't quite get my mind around the fact that he had also elected to become a hit-and-run driver. He held the door open for me. "Come on!" he said. "It's on me—this is your send off."

"Great," I said.

I walked inside and we found a place to sit. My stomach was roiling with bile. There was no need, of course, to wonder where a good gastroenterologist was when you needed one: back home, obviously, in Somerset, PA.

Tuttle found a menu and a pretty waitress came by. We ordered, and I asked Tuttle if he wasn't the least bit concerned, given our proximity to the scene of the crime.

"Nah," he said. "The guy deserved it."

"Right," I said, not too convincingly. I had a schedule to keep, a hotel to reach by midnight. I didn't need an angry power forward from a professional basketball team chasing my truck all the way to Chattanooga. Still, I liked Tuttle—we had had many adventures together over the years, one or two of them extreme, thanks to Tuttle, who made expansive small talk while I nodded. Something about his wife, something about his dissertation, something about Florida. I nodded and watched the window, said yeah and uh-huh until my sausage and eggs arrived, a stack of pancakes. Tuttle got a strawberry, whipped cream thing with three silver dollar pancakes on the bottom. He had to dig to find them but took to it with the avidity of a treasure hunter. I prodded my eggs, shoving them about the plate, and thought of the road, the hours of driving, my cat caterwauling all down through the Midwest and South. Tuttle ate blissfully, and then I looked out into the parking lot and saw the owner of the Benz. He and a police officer were looking at Tuttle's car. Then they looked toward the restaurant.

"We should leave as soon as we can," I said.

I had eaten maybe three or four bites—my stomach was still queasy—but Tuttle, chewing industriously, was half-way through. "Why?" he said, bits of pancake coating his teeth.

"The Benz owner is out there, and he's got a cop."

"Screw 'em," Tuttle said, and continued to eat.

"Is this part of your I've-got-nothing-to-live-for thing?" I asked. Tuttle's wife, a marine biologist, had left him the year before for a research grant in New Zealand. He hadn't seen her in all that time and had become a different man. Road rage was just the latest of his sins.

"Yep," he said.

"Fine, but I have a job to go to, and a life to live, so excuse me and I'm going to have to leave." I held out my hand and we shook. "Thanks for everything," I said. "The boat rides, the conversation, the pool playing—I appreciate all of it."

"You're welcome," Tuttle said. "Be sure to write."

"I will," I said.

"That's better than some people," he said. He meant his wife.

"She doesn't write?"

"Hardly ever," he said.

I could see the Benz owner and the cop headed inside.

"See you," I said.

"Yep," Tuttle said. He took a meditative bite, his head slowly nodding. For a second, I wondered what my father would have done, but it occurred to me that he'd never have gotten himself into such a situation to begin with—his entire life had militated against making wrong choices, like a chess player determined never to lose. I passed the Benz owner and the cop, my face just as blank as a napkin as they stepped inside. Neither one looked at me, and as I started down the handicap ramp from I-HOP I thought that Tuttle could take care of himself—he'd argue it was an accident, he didn't know he hit the car, and say he was sorry, and with that honest face of his, they'd let him go and he'd settle with the man out of court, pay him a few hundred or a thousand—his wife would send the money, if need be. She still did that much for him, though otherwise, she wanted nothing else to do with him.

I walked up Harper to my old apartment building and spotted the truck. I stood on its door step and looked in the window at the cat, who was turning around in her case, making herself comfortable. I started to get inside the cab, but I hesitated. I looked up at the old building. Jacintha was home, her windows open, the shades up. There was time, I told myself, so I buzzed her apartment and she buzzed me in.

"Dr. Patel," she said as I reached the third floor. "I am honored."

"Dr. Singh," I said. "Good to see you once again."

We had graduated in June, she in economics. We were the only ones who used our titles, and we did so ironically and discreetly— it was a little awkward around others like Nielsen, who might never finish, and Tuttle, who had yet to defend.

"Sorry about last night," I said.

"You mean the girl Nielsen brought home?"

"Yeah."

"I'm used to it," she said. "That's why I put my bedroom above yours."

"Thanks a lot," I said.

Jacintha laughed gently, reassuring me. "Would you like a cup of coffee?" she asked.

"Sure," I said. "That would be great."

She had taken me out the night before to a Chinese restaurant called the House of Eng. We had sat on its tenth floor patio and looked out on Lake Michigan. At dusk the sailboats were out, the color of the water shifting, the park between us shifting, too, from Chicago students to neighborhood folk, boom boxes sounding. The chicken curry was excellent but we didn't say much during the meal, and once we got back to the building our goodbye had been muted, as if it were just any occasion, not one more special. I had thought it would amount to more.

She was glad to see me again, regardless, and we sat at her table and she made me fresh coffee, from the bean. The sari was long gone, jeans and a sweat top replacing it, bare feet, more her style. I told her the morning's story about Tuttle, and she laughed. "Wow, you sure know some guys," she said.

"Should I have stuck around?" I asked. "To back up his story?"

She squinted her eyes and thought. "No," she said. "Tuttle can take care of himself. He talks a smoother line than Nielsen."

I had known Jacintha nearly the whole time I lived in Chicago. She was dark and pretty, but not that tall. I towered over her. Her father was a scholar of South Asian languages at the university, a translator and a poet. Her mother was a novelist, and though they were immigrants they had raised their daughter, born in the States, to be a Hyde Parker through and through: Lab School and soccer team, U of C undergrad and grad, parties and receptions at the Quadrangle Club.

"Hungry?" she asked.

"Definitely," I said. "I've had maybe four bites of food all day."

"I know," she said. "I was listening to your story."

She made me spaghetti. Nothing fancy. Just Ragu and some Mueller's. She unwrapped a half pound chunk of Romano—real cheese, which she grated over the top for me.

"That smells great," I said.

"I love this stuff," she said.

She kept a beautiful apartment. Her front window had plants on little stands and plants hanging all along, all of them healthy. Her floors were sanded and waxed and always shiny clean. Her kitchen was immaculate. Her dining room furniture was the closest thing to real furniture of all the friends I knew. Her parents' place, on Kenwood near 57th, was just as nice. No, nicer. They threw elaborate parties sometimes, artists and movie stars from India attending. I always felt just a little out of place, especially when someone like Ramanujan or Chandrashaker showed up. They were giants, but not to Jacintha, who had grown up with them and called them uncle.

My stomach had calmed down from my earlier adrenalin rush at Tuttle's car-bashing. We ate and then she fixed us each another plate. It was easy to be around her, just a way she had. The first time we ever really talked was my first winter in Chicago. She was walking ahead of me on the street, carrying groceries through half a foot of snow. I wanted to ask if she needed help and I kept trying to catch up to her, which I did, finally, but not till we had reached the lobby of our building. I walked in right behind her and scared her, but then she could see who I was between my cap and scarf. "You're the boy from my methods class," she said. "Yeah," I said. "How did you remember?" She laughed. "Because you're like the only other Indian in all of Social Sciences," she said. "If you haven't noticed, most are in Physics, or Math, or South Asian Studies over in Humanities." "Or in Med School," I said. She nodded. We both laughed then, and she let me help carry her groceries up the stairs. I trailed snow inside her place; she handed me a mop. "Even Indian boys are slobs," she said. "Seriously, what is it with guys not wiping their feet?"

We sat eating the spaghetti, a nice Indian boy in the home of a lovely Indian girl, two old friends. My mother, I know, would have killed for a photograph of that scene. But she would have to content herself with my doctor sister, pregnant at the time, with a doctor husband and a thirty-year mortgage on their four-bedroom home, in Harrisburg, instead.

At 1:30, Jacintha noticed the clock. "Oh," she said. "I have a paper to finish for a talk Monday morning." It was half done, but she had more numbers to crunch, tables to fill, works to cite. She would send me a copy when it was published, the way she always shared her work with me.

"Thank you," I said. "I look forward to reading it."

"What about your cat?" she suddenly asked. "Is she okay in that truck out there?" Jacintha sat for her sometimes on those rare occasions when both Nielsen and I were out of town. She said she liked doing it—it was like owning your own cat but not really having to put up with the fuss.

"She'll be all right," I said. "I left the windows open just a crack. It's not that warm out today."

"No, it never is," she said.

"The windy city," I said. And then we sat there saying nothing for a long time. We were done with the meal. "I have to go," I said at last.

"Just leave like it was any other day," she said. "Not like you were leaving town for good, but like you were just going back downstairs to your place."

"Why?" I said.

"Just do it for me," she said. I didn't know then that she had been in love with me. Nielsen would tell me years later, after she had left Chicago for Seattle. She was a good friend, always, someone who would listen to what I had to say, listen close and tell me what she thought. If I had been a shit, she'd let me know, just as she'd let me know if I had done good that day. She was wise—wiser than me, than anyone I knew.

"Then, I'll see you later," I said. I stood up.

"See you later," she said, standing.

I did not hug her and I certainly did not kiss her. I had never done either in all the years I knew her, and to do so then would have been a betrayal. The moment when things might have been different came early in our knowing one another, and the moment passed, neither of us acting on it, so there we were, old friends, and old friends only. I waved bye and she closed the door and latched it, the way she always did. I walked past my old apartment door and kept going down the stairs, and I walked out into the sunlight and got in the truck. My cat was sleeping in her box. She looked peaceful and content. I started up the truck and pulled away. At 79th Street, I caught the Skyway. I kept going, deep into Indiana, all the way down into Tennessee.

I called Jacintha when I got to my hotel room, but there was no answer. I left a message, said hey, named the hotel and the town. It was just as well that I missed her, I thought. This made things easier for us both. My cat and I sat on the bed in that hotel room and I played with her awhile and fed her packaged tuna. There was no one in the room but us, and nothing much in the room besides a bed, a TV, and a swivel chair. Everything I owned in the world was on the truck outside. I looked out the window and saw it sitting in the moonlight—the same moon shining over Chicago, where I had lived for eight long years, and over the state of Florida, where I was bound. For all I knew, Jacintha, Nielsen, and Tuttle had met up somewhere at a bar and were having a late-night drink, toasting my new life. She had put aside her numbers, Nielsen had decided to go celibate if only for the night, and Tuttle was talking to them about his new best friend, a power forward for the Chicago Bulls. Stranger things have happened in this world. At midnight the phone rang and it was her.

"Let me talk to the cat," she said.

OAK PARK, ILLINOIS

So there we are kneeling on the bed, I mean right in the middle, when Baldwin's kid steps into the room. Baldwin's body goes rigid, then he pushes me away.

What are you doing? says his son.

Nothing, Baldwin says, trying to adjust his clothes. We're not doing anything, he adds, his voice high pitched, choked, like he might cry.

You are too, says the kid, who's maybe six, maybe seven—I can't tell, not having been around kids for so long a time.

Baldwin jumps up and turns his back to us. He's still wearing his trenchcoat, dressed like some goddam spy who likes to keep things fast, efficient. You can see his elbows flying around there and he's bending over, moving like one of those escape artists you see in the streets, locked up in cheap chains and squirming on the pavement, an empty hat hoping for money. What the hell are you doing home anyway, Baldwin shouts over his shoulder. Then he turns angrily and faces his kid. Baldwin's belt's only half in place, a shirttail working through his fly.

The kid looks angry, too, like this primal scene is working on him. Ten years from now he won't remember the details, I bet, but he won't forget the feeling of this day. He starts breathing like a locomotive, like a bull that snorts in some old Warner Bros. cartoon. I'm telling Mom, he shouts, and apparently it's not exactly the right thing to say to Baldwin, whose face loses color.

What would you tell her, he says, like it's a dare and it's two six-year-olds having it out right here in front of me. I roll my eyes toward the window and the hazy sky, see a jetplane heading for O'Hare. I try to picture things from Baldwin's point of view, think what it's like to have your kid catch you fucking some teenager at mid-morning on a business day. It's a stretch, though, because even if I ever do have kids, Baldwin's not exactly the kind of Dad I'd want to be. Then from the corner of my eye I see a paperweight fly across the room, see it catch Baldwin right in the shirttail, the kid standing now by Baldwin's desk and staring at his felled prey. Baldwin's on his knees, his cheeks turning from green to red, his teeth chewing his fat tongue. They just stare at one another.

So should I leave you two alone or what, I say.

Go sit in the car, Joe, Baldwin says in some red-faced, tongue-chewing voice not his own.

No one does or says anything for a good five seconds. Baldwin and his son drill each other with thick pupils, and then he looks my way, his eyes fix me this time. I said, Baldwin says, sounding like I'd better get my ass in motion, for you to get in the car—that same purple tone, the words with spaces between them. I straighten up fast, stand up and walk past the kid. Talk to you later, I say, as much to his kid as to Baldwin, pulling shut the door as I exit, thinking this shit now is not my problem.

I walk down the stairs with all its plush carpeting, head off through the kitchen and grab myself a Danish that's sitting on the table—just lying there, round with plenty of gooey sugar smeared across it, cream cheese filling. It's calling me, so I take it through the kitchen door and on in to the garage, which smells like gasoline and motor oil, dried grass on the underside of Baldwin's riding mower, from when the grass was growing still. Not like now, all the snow lying out there on top of everything. I tell myself, as I get inside the car, I wish I had some water.

Baldwin's Lexus has two thousand controls on the driver's panel, like maybe the thing would fly if you drove it down a runway. It's white, the whole thing. White outside and pale interior, pale carpeting, pale seats. The whiteness catches what little light there is seeping in through the bottom of the garage door, and after a minute—after eating that Danish, too (and wiping my hands on the side of the car seat)—my eyes adjust and I get to study all the tools Baldwin keeps inside his suburban garage. Stuff for his car— jumper cables, a battery recharger, cans of motor oil—and for the lawn, the driveway—blacktop, snow blower.

And there's kid stuff in that garage, too, the tricycle, the training wheeled bicycle, and hanging on the wall the junior trail bike with fat tires. There's even another big fat parking space for his missus's car, with nice, dark oil drips lying beneath where her car's engine goes. I'll have to tell Baldwin—when he comes down from telling Junior some big lie about what daddy was doing with that nice young man—say hey, you know, you should crawl under your wife's oil pan and take a look. She's leaking, pal, and bad, too, it looks like. And I'm thinking about what it is she probably drives when Baldwin bursts through the doorway into the garage, looking like something very awful has just happened. He leaves the garage door wide open and he's got his keys in his hand and jumps inside the car so fast he doesn't bother trying to shut his door. He grinds the engine, keeps the key going too long in the ignition.

You'll get fumes inside your house, I say.

Doesn't matter, he says, flooding his engine.

Stop that, I say.

What? he says above the racket

Stop grinding the fucking engine. You're killing your car.

But he doesn't stop, and I have to reach over and turn his key hand back, make him stop with the engine.

Baldwin's shaking all at once, and then he wraps his arms around his trench-coated self and says I killed him, I killed my son.

He rocks back and forth, touching the steering wheel almost and then rocking back in the seat until his haircut touches the headrest. There's a flood of light coming from the kitchen that illuminates the front end of the car, striking the far wall of the garage, too, and I see his cutting tools then, the stuff he uses to trim his lawn, to cut it, slash it. Maybe he burns it, for all I know, looking at the big gasoline can in the corner. Uses those controlled burns come the fall, maybe, and if I went outside to his back yard right now and shoveled away all the snow, maybe I'd find burned grass, brown, curled at the end. I'd tear some away with the shovel, sure, but there'd be enough still on the ground so you could tell how he did it, controlled the growth, I mean. Kept things from getting out of hand.

What do you mean, I say, hearing myself say it, like my head is inside a drain pipe, the sound of my voice so strange.

With the pillow, he says. Over his face.

Where?

He doesn't answer. He rocks instead. Touching the headrest, then the steering wheel, the headrest again. He looks like a goddam bob, or like one of those clown balloons little kids slap away at. He's been wrong before about things, Baldwin. Given to panic I guess, like upstairs earlier when his kid caught us—a lot of men could handle that one, make something up about daddy practicing his wrestling moves with this fit young man, the kind of thing a six year old would want to believe. But Baldwin would rather lose it than be smooth.

I'll take a look, I say. Maybe he's not dead.

He's dead! Baldwin screams. Don't go look, it's too awful. And then he rocks some more like the big baby he is.

Whatever, Baldwin, I say, fine. And so we sit there, the two of us, me thinking how much I'd rather be in any other home out this way, with any other man but Baldwin. Somebody single, maybe, no wife, no kids—but then again, why would such a man live out here? I make a mental note to quit walking West Roosevelt, where Baldwin always finds me. There's plenty of other streets in a city like Chicago. Finally I say I could use some water—my ruse to get back inside, but only half a ruse, parts of that Danish still clinging to my throat.

Baldwin tells me the glasses are in the cabinet to the left of the sink. I say thank you and he says you're welcome as I step outside the car. Inside I turn out the kitchen light—it's too bright somehow, making everything seem too real. The sink has one of those Price-Pfister faucets, the regular kind not good enough, I guess, for the sparkling stuff tax payer dollars pay for out this way, suburban tap. I drink some and realize it's the first water I've had all morning, so I tell myself I've got to watch that sort of thing, tell myself water is important, you can't drink too much, and what you don't need you get rid of down some alley. Maybe you hit the john at the public library if they don't know you, don't think you're up to something in there that might disturb the patrons. Joe, I hear Baldwin say from the garage. The rest of the house is eerily quiet, and I don't much like it. Joe? he says again, this time with a question mark after my name. I can't keep myself from wondering about the kid.

As I pass through the hallway the phone rings twice and then the answering machine comes on. It is Baldwin's missus and the call is for little Robby—not for Baldwin, who should be at work. Mommy says to little Robby she's sorry she couldn't stay home with him this morning, but now her boss has said she can come home so now she is in fact coming home and she will pick up orange juice and Pop Tarts at the store so little Robby can eat those and feel all better. She sounds like a nice woman, really, probably a good mom but for this morning's lapse of no babysitter on too short a notice.

I walk up the stairs, taking my time, not wanting, really, to get to the top too fast. I start noticing the family portraits as I go up,

noticing that there seems to be a portrait of the three of them—
Baldwin, his wife, their son—for every birthday the kid has had,
like the stairwell is their monument to his aging. Each picture is
the same pose, mom to little Robby's left and dad to his right,
cake out front, all three of them working at the candles with their
lips. The table is the same one as downstairs, the pictures being
snapped, I guess, by whatever muchacha it is that Baldwin is not
paying Social Security on that year. The pictures go only halfway
up the stairs and stop at seven candles.

On the second floor there are four rooms, each with its door
pulled to. I am holding back on going in to Baldwin's room,
since, really, I can do without seeing his son just lying there, his
eyes open, maybe, or maybe closed. I push wide the door anyway
and look at the bed, see that it's empty. Oh that's the bed all right,
it's all messed up from where I was on it before, and there's a fat
pillow, dead center, but no sign of little Robby. I walk around the
bed to look at the side against the wall, thinking that somehow
Baldwin might've knocked the kid to the floor, but again there's
nothing. Then I'm on my knees looking under the bed, on the off
chance that maybe in his dying throes Robby crawled under there,
if such a thing could ever be. I try not to get spooked, wondering if
Baldwin has dragged the kid somewhere, tried to hide him, maybe,
but the closet is empty except for Baldwin's clothes, nice suits, all
Brooks. Wing-tipped shoes line the floor.

The next room I try is the room of Baldwin's missus, and
somehow I'd missed that, that the two of them kept separate
rooms. It's woman's stuff, all of it, her dresser lined with bottle
after bottle of perfume, make-up, and pills, at least a dozen
prescriptions, Valium, Librium. Now it's a kind of tour I'm on,
the guest room next, pictures of old folks who are doubtless little
Robby's grandparents, both sets looking like Chicago Gothic.
Last comes Robby's room. I push the door open slowly, see that
he's sitting before his homework desk nice and wholesome, not

propped up by a crazed father or anything like that, but alive and breathing, staring, of all things, at a picture of Baldwin dressed in a baseball uniform, his bat cocked, his eye looking right into the camera's.

Don't burn your eyes out, kid, I say, and he turns and looks at me with dry eyes, though his nose is bleeding.

I'm pretty glad to see that Baldwin was altogether wrong about having killed the kid. I figured he hadn't really done it—he's the type who'd not remember right a scene where he's trying to suffocate his own kid. He wouldn't think, after, to check for any kind of pulse; to hold a mirror beneath the kid's nose. He should watch more TV, I think; it could do a whole lot for that style of his.

How come, Robby says.

How come what, I say.

How come you know my father?

He's just a friend, I say, and Robby looks at me hard, so I try again: He's just a man I met, that's all.

I get him a Kleenex from his desk and hand it to him and tell him to wipe, which he does, which gives him something to do and so he seems to feel better, a little more in control maybe. He drops the Kleenex into a little trash can beside his desk. He looks at me, afraid. He looks away and runs his hands across some books on his desktop, and then Robby tells me what I already know, that daddy put a pillow over his face. He tells me he had to lie very still, so daddy would take the pillow away. He tells me he had to lie that way for a long time, till daddy screamed goddam and then ran from the room, all this in a kind of robot voice. He wasn't really sick this morning, he tells me, he only pretended.

You're pretty good at pretending, I say, smiling a little.

What do you mean? he says.

Well, I say, you fooled mommy this morning about being sick—Robby nods and grins—And you fooled daddy just a while ago, in his room on the bed—

But then Robby's eyes grow wide like tangerines, so I ask him quickly about that picture of Baldwin, ask Robby does he play ball, too, and if so what position. I mean, what can you say to a kid who's been killed and come back? Not really killed, of course, but the things inside him have been. He starts telling me he only plays whiffle ball out back sometimes with dad, who plays in a summer league for his company.

Yeah, I say, it's probably a swell way for dad to meet other men, and by the look on Robby's face, I can see he has half an idea what it is I mean, and he doesn't look too happy. It's just a joke, Robby, I say. I say I didn't mean it, but he keeps looking at me like he knows I did.

I tell Robby why doesn't he just hang out up here for a while, and I tell him, too, that his mom called a few minutes ago and said she'd be home soon. I tell him she's bringing him Pop Tarts and orange juice, and for half a second he looks happy. Just stay up here, I say. You can maybe hide in your closet, if you want, till your mom gets home.

He looks scared for me to be leaving, but I pat his head and take off, wanting to get to the garage before Baldwin has a chance to do anything really stupid. He's shut the kitchen door, I find when I get down there, and I open up the garage and see that the room is dark. I run my hand along the wall until I find the light switch. He's sitting on the floor, right where his wife's car goes, doubtless ruining his coat by wiping his ass along the oil stains.

So what are you doing?

Take my keys, he says.

He's holding them in the air for me.

Why should I do that, I ask, and he tells me he's thinking of driving out to the Eisenhower the wrong way and running head-on into a truck.

What kind of truck, I say, but he doesn't answer my smart remark. The keys rattle in his hand, impatient for me. It stinks in here, I think, it smelling like every kind of engine fluid a garage could have.

Inside the kitchen I open wide the back door and the window above the sink, to keep the smell from getting inside the rest of the house. All this life-saving starts making me tired, so I find a cup and pour myself some cold coffee from the Mr. C., put that in the microwave on two minutes. Baldwin walks in just before the coffee is done, looks at me, turns toward the cabinet to find himself a cup and, indeed, he's oiled up not only the seat of his trenchcoat, but the elbows, too. Don't worry, I say, you can write it off on your insurance.

He whips around, stricken, and I realize he thinks I mean his son. Your coat, I say. I mean your goddam coat. Oh, shit, Baldwin, don't cry.

I don't cry, he says.

No, I say. You just look like you're about to ninety percent of the time, and then he looks even more hurt, if that's possible.

The microwave beeps and I walk over to get my coffee, take a sip—it's good, definitely not just something from out of a supermarket tin can. It's hot against my tongue, and Baldwin's keys dig into my leg inside my pocket.

I called for you, he says to me. I called for you twice, but you didn't answer.

I had things to do, I say, blowing on the coffee.

But you did hear me calling you, he says.

Sure, I say. The first time you just said my name, kind of flat. Like this: Joe. The second time there was a question to it: Joe?—like that. Did you need me or something?

Baldwin's holding an empty cup now and is looking at me.

You know, I say, back in old Greece they had to take their kids out to some mountain and chain them to a rock or something. I guess they didn't have pillows back then, huh?

He rears back and flings the cup at me. I watch it sail past and hear it break against the wall. I doubt they let him pitch out there in summer league. Not with a sissy throw like that. I sip my coffee, ignore him.

Your wife'll be home in a few minutes, I say.

She's at work, he says dully.

No, I say. She's coming home any minute. She left a message on the machine saying so.

He knows I'm not lying.

You'd better think up some story, I say. About the boy, I mean.

Baldwin walks over and sits, heavily, at the breakfast table. He puts his head in his hands, having to hold it up.

Boy, I say. I'm glad I'm not you. He looks about to cry again, but he was being truthful when he said he didn't cry, because surely he'd cry now, being so needled by me as he is. I actually start to feel sorry for the sonofabitch. I can't quite bring myself to tell him his son's as good at pretending as he is, but I figure maybe I can edge somewhere close to the truth. So, Baldwin, I say.

Yes?

I take it you wish you hadn't done what you did.

Yes, he says, the single word sounding about as profound as it can, being said as it is by someone so despairing.

Do you believe in miracles, Baldwin? I ask him.

He thinks about it. He thinks for a long time, then finally he says no.

That's too bad, I say. Too fucking bad. I finish my coffee. It's cold by now, all the cold air coming in from the kitchen door and window. Then his wife pulls in the driveway, right on cue. You can just see the top of her car, a green Forester, from where I am standing, and then the garage door rolls open, and a wall of cold air and engine fumes races through the kitchen and out the door, the window. I reach into my pocket and grab Baldwin's keys. Here, I say, tossing them—they hit him in the face, but he doesn't seem to feel it. Oh, shit, I say, I thought you'd try to catch them.

He just sits there looking like someone who thinks he killed his son, a drop of blood now on his cheek. I walk to the back door as I hear his wife's car roll to a halt inside the garage. Baldwin, I say, he's okay. He's alive still, so don't do anything crazy. But Baldwin looks at me then, and I can see by his face he's not sure whether to believe me. You're so fucking cruel, he says.

Baldwin, are you home? his wife, from the garage, calls out, and I head out the doorway into their snowy backyard. There's a whiffle bat leaning against the side of the house, and a lump of snow beside it that probably hides the ball. I keep moving, around the side of Baldwin's garage and out onto the shoveled suburban sidewalk, the rush of Chicago-bound traffic coming from the thoroughfare at the end of the street.

OLD SCHOOL

All Wesley had wanted in life was a friend, a good friend, someone he could trust. Someone he could play ball with and sit down for a beer some nights to pour out his heart. He had a lot of pain. He'd just lost his wife of fifteen years—divorce—and that hurt so bad he couldn't even speak of it. Just after that his best friend's wife, Victoria, had tried to get him into bed, and there went that, Allan, the one best friend he'd had, because the bitch had lied about just what it was that took place, and who did what to whom. He lost them both, his best friend, his wife, in the same year. And then a whole year passed, Wesley alone for much of it, just him and his seventh-graders; teaching kept him busy in the daytime, but the nights stretched pretty long before him.

Much of the time he just sat there in his one-bedroom Chicago apartment, half his things not even there, his CDs, his DVDs, his books—still back with his wife in boxes in the basement of their townhouse. Just Wesley and some beige walls, a piece or two of furniture. He got out some nights down the street to Jimmy's, a corner bar in Hyde Park near the University. Jimmy's was loud, the food was greasy, but the beer was beer. He'd have one or two of those, maybe a bratwurst, some sauerkraut. Maybe a Reuben, some fries, another beer. He sat by himself at the bar.

People tried to talk to him; usually he ignored them. He had a right to be like this, he thought. The kind of thing he'd say to an interloper there at the bar, on a stool, was something like, "Hey, can't a man eat his goddam sandwich and drink his goddam beer in peace?" He watched TV, the moving pictures and the type print that scrolled across the bottom of the screen, most of it about killings and disasters. The Iraq War stories often depressed him; fighting in the Sudan made him want to cry. The home-mortgage crisis might have been the worst thing, however, and after he'd had enough of watching families standing in the street beside their ex-houses, he'd stare into space. A long mirror hung behind the bar and Wesley studied it some nights, the movements of the patrons. He saw his own mocha self, tall, thin, flecks of grey, and then he scanned out to his right awhile and then out to his left, first near, then deep. Jimmy's had all kinds of characters—neighborhood, university, some petit crime doers and some hustlers into big economic scams. You could find almost any kind of person in that place.

Then at Jimmy's one night, near the one-year anniversary of his divorce, Wesley saw Victoria. Long red hair, big green eyes, full hips, tight dress, long legs, just past forty, she was unmistakable. Nobody else looked like her, at least nobody he'd ever seen. She was with a black man half her age, a table in the corner of the room. Two empty glasses sat pushed aside, two full ones waiting, the young man lighting her cigarette and then his own, staring into her eyes like he was Billy Dee Williams or someone equally as smooth. Wesley wished he had a cell phone that took pictures, so he could point the phone Victoria's way, click the photo and then send it to his ex-friend Allan. It gave him a grim satisfaction to imagine Allan seeing the truth about his wife.

But there was also a young man beside Wesley that night, a white guy, trying to tell him jokes which Wesley at first was able to ignore with half a smile and something like a nod. He wanted to spy on Victoria undisturbed.

"I got a Catholic joke, if you're interested," the guy beside him said.

Wesley ignored him.

"Presbyterian? Anglican?"

Wesley slapped his hand on the bar, and the guy shut up.

In the mirror Wesley watched Victoria and Billie Dee, saw Victoria's hand slip under the table and stay there, Billie looking into her eyes and smiling. Not long after that they got up. Wesley kept his head down and watched in the mirror as Victoria and Billie walked past, Victoria oblivious to his presence, her eyes stuck on her escort, her arm through his, both smiling.

The guy beside Wesley watched Wesley's eyes in the mirror. He watched them watch the couple walking out the door.

"Hey, who is she?" he asked.

Wesley looked in the mirror. "What's it to you?" he said, and the guy just raised his eyebrows, looking hurt.

"It's nothing to me, really," he said. "Just trying to talk." He went back to his beer, and Wesley drank his own beer down and took a quick look at the talker. In his twenties, it looked like, and Wesley had double that under his own belt. New in town or something, on top of that, but Wesley didn't know. He had big eyes and the thickest eyebrows Wesley had ever seen. It was okay he was there, Wesley decided, as long as he didn't speak. Wesley turned to the window, waiting for Victoria's car to pass. And then it did, she driving by in her Town Car, Billie Dee squeezed right beside her, his lips smashed up against her cheek. "No surprise," Wesley muttered, turning back to face ahead.

He ordered another beer. And then one more. The TV continued—talking heads, smiling faces, words that crawled beneath them, world news and a sixteen-year-old Somali pirate, grinning at the camera, being taken into U.S. custody. Finally Wesley ordered a beer for the road. He'd been on a foreign tour of sorts: Dos Equis, Grolsch, St. Pauli Girl, and Moosehead. The green bottle sat before him on the bar, the brown moose in profile.

"Which one do you like best?" he heard the young man, the persistent young man beside him, ask. Wesley had almost forgotten him, and he smiled into the mirror. "The one with the girl on the label," he said. The guy laughed like it was the funniest thing he'd ever heard. His big grin and friendly face came up close, telling Wesley a joke about a Jew named Goldberg and a Chinaman named Huang, and Wesley, who disliked ethnic jokes, laughed anyway. He took a big long drink of his Moosehead.

The guy pointed to the label. "If that moose could talk, huh?" he said.

Wesley laughed.

"Okay, you going to tell me who she is?"

Wesley nodded. "Just an old friend," he said.

"A *good* friend?" He winked at Wesley.

"No, just an old friend who tried to get me into bed," Wesley said.

"So what's wrong with that?"

"She was married."

"So?"

"To my best friend," Wesley said.

The young man nodded. "That's a good reason not to get in the sack."

"You bet."

They didn't say anything for a few moments. They watched the patrons in the room, then they watched some TV, the news or an infomercial, Wesley couldn't tell which. He was pretty drunk by then.

"Can I ask you something?" the young man said.

"Sure," Wesley said.

"What was her move?"

"Her *move*?"

"Yeah," he said. "What did she do?"

"Lap dance," Wesley said.

The young man laughed.

"A lap dance?"

Wesley nodded.

"Where were you? In a strip joint?"

"In her living room."

"Where was your best friend?"

"Away on business."

"Okay, then, why were you there?"

Wesley looked straight ahead at the mirror, saying nothing, studying his own face. It floated above a row of whiskey bottles, a basket of fries, a Chicago Bears T-shirt one of the bartenders was using for a bar swipe. Wesley signaled the bartender, to get another Moose.

"Sorry, man," he heard the young man say.

Wesley got his new Moose and the guy launched into a joke about a zebra and a walrus who somehow end up in a shower stall. At least that's how Wesley would remember it. He bought Wesley one more beer, which Wesley only took a sip of, and then he drove him home, because Wesley had said he was too drunk to drive. He played Wesley some Coltrane on the way over, "My Favorite Things." "1960," the young man said—"listen to that horn!"

Wesley listened, though he'd heard the cut many times before. They passed Kimbark Liquor, a food co-op, a hardware store.

"What do you think?" he said, pointing to his CD player.

"I think you're kind of old school for a young man," Wesley said, and the young man laughed.

"You have a name?" Wesley asked.

"Larry."

They were just outside Wesley's building, and Wesley pointed Larry toward the back of it, a parking spot beside his own empty space in front of the dumpster. "Wesley," he said. "My name is Wesley."

They shook, Larry's car engine running. Wesley thought of his apartment, the empty rooms. "Look, you want a beer?" he said. "I mean, nothing funny, seriously. I'm not like that. But I could use a friend."

Larry looked at him. "Hey," he said. "I understand. Totally. It's a big, bad city. South Side and all that—and for the record, I didn't think you were 'like that.' Seriously."

"Cool?"

"Cool."

Once they got inside the building, the walk down the hallway wasn't bad—Wesley almost had his balance by then, and his key wasn't all that hard to fish from his pocket. Inside his apartment, the phone was flashing five times. "Hit that machine," Wesley said, lying on the couch and at this point just half drunk.

The first message was from Victoria. She told Wesley she missed him, said she wanted to see him. She never told Allan a damn thing, she said. And she was drunk, both Wesley and Larry could tell, as they listened.

"She's a lying stack of shit," Wesley said.

"'Victoria,'" Larry said. "That's quite a name."

"Yeah," Wesley said, "and she insists on the whole thing, no short versions."

"No Vicky," the young man said.

"No Vic or Victor or Vixen," Wesley smiled.

The second message, mid-stream by then, was his mother saying come by for dinner on Sunday. (It was Saturday night, she reminded him, in case he was losing track of the days—Wesley rolled his eyes.) His mother also told him to go to church in the morning, saying it would do him good. Larry laughed and said Wesley didn't seem to him like the church-going type, whatever that was.

The third message was Allan, asking if Victoria was there. He sounded angry.

"Strange shit," Wesley said. "She must've told her husband she was going out to look for me this evening."

"Your old friend?" Larry said, and Wesley nodded.

The fourth message was Victoria. Again. She said she was lonely. She was driving around in her car. She'd seen Wesley back at Jimmy's, drinking all those beers. "I know you think I didn't see you," she said, "but I did. Call me, on my cell as soon as you can." She gave the number, in case Wesley had forgotten.

"Bitch," Wesley said. The machine said the message had come in at 12:02 A.M.; it was 12:30 by this point.

The fifth message was a long sigh—Victoria's—and then a hang-up. The machine beeped for the last time.

"Damn," Wesley said. He was beat. Part of it was the beer, part of it Victoria. He closed his eyes and heard the young man wander into the kitchen, and then he came back with two Buds from Wesley's refrigerator. Wesley took one and the two men sipped, staring at one another.

"Nice place," Larry said.

"It's home," Wesley said.

"You married?"

"Was. You?"

"Was."

They laughed.

"What's your story?" Wesley asked.

"Wife woke up one morning and said she hated me. Said she hated what a slob I was, how I was always late for everything, and how my grammar sucked. You?"

Wesley looked at him, shook his head, said, "She left me for a younger man." And that was all he said. Larry returned his look, and then he held his bottle out to Wesley, and Wesley looked at the young man's bottle and then raised his bottle too—each pointed the bottle toward the other, and then they drank.

The phone rang. "Guess who this is," Wesley said. It was Victoria, saying she was parked out back of Wesley's building. "Go let her in," Wesley said. Larry did. He went to let her in the back door of the building and Wesley imagined that young Larry would see how good she looked in her high heels and tight skirt—her uniform, practically speaking—and then he thought about how she'd looked earlier, in the corner back at Jimmy's. Unique.

"I need to talk to Wesley," he could hear Victoria say, loudly, as she walked down the corridor toward his place. And then she was in the room, standing there with Larry. It seemed like a long, long time since this had happened, Victoria standing in a place where he lived, this time without Allan. Larry helped her take off her fancy coat, clearly smitten with what he saw.

"Shut the door," Wesley said, trying to muster up a smile. "I got neighbors I don't want to disturb."

"Fuck the neighbors, Wesley. Wherever you live, you always worry about the neighbors," Victoria said.

"I'm funny that way," he said. "And you're drunk—anyone ever tell you that?"

"Pot calling the kettle black," she said. Then added: "And I mean nothing by that, so don't play any cards with me."

"Speaking of which," Wesley said, "what'd you do with that young man I saw you with earlier?"

Victoria looked at him. "He's just a friend, Wesley. I gave him a ride home."

"I bet you did."

"Fuck you, Wesley." She looked around the room, taking in all the nothing. "Jesus, Wesley. This is how you live? Remind me to take you to a furniture store sometime."

"It's minimalism," Wesley said, but already Victoria wasn't listening.

Larry stared at her like some playful puppy as she dropped her purse on the floor and put on some Miles Davis and danced alone in the center of the room, lost in her own world, it seemed—whatever it was she had come to say, she didn't say. She danced instead. Wesley drank his beer and watched the young man watching Victoria dance, and Wesley smiled to himself and shook his head. They finished off the Bud. They went through all of Wesley's beer and then, already drunk, they found a bottle of champagne in the back of the refrigerator's crisper. And that was about the last thing Wesley remembered. He fell asleep on the couch, and in the morning, early, he found Victoria and the young man naked in his bed. "If this don't beat the shit," he said. They both wore those little pointed caps people wore on New Year's, and Wesley had a vague remembrance of finding them in a package in the back of a cabinet, leftovers from the night his divorce was final, even though he drank that night alone. He reached up and pulled his own pointy cap off his head.

His phone rang once, and then a second time, and he picked it up in the next room, figuring it was his mother calling to bug him about church. It was Allan.

"Wesley," Allan said.

"Speaking," Wesley said, going on rote, wondering how this would play out.

"Have you seen my wife?"

"Yeah," Wesley, never a liar, said.

"Recently?"

"Sure."

"Put her on."

Wesley paused.

"Put her on the goddam phone!" Allan shouted, and Wesley said sure, you're the man.

He took the phone to the bedroom. The ringing had not awakened them, Larry looking as muscular and young as Victoria looked soft and middle-aged. He reached down and nudged the curve of her ass through his blankets, saying someone on the phone. She tried to sit up and looked into Wesley's eyes. They stared at one another briefly, then she glanced at the number and then glared at Wesley, snatching the phone. "Yeah?" she said. Lots of silence, at least on Wesley's end, as he stood there watching. Some more yeahs and some uh-huhs, and she told Allan she'd be home in an hour. She took her cap off and looked at Wesley.

"I need to use your shower," she said, and Wesley said he thought that was a fine idea. She pushed past him and slammed the door.

Wesley was awake enough at that point to realize two things: he was hungry and he had a headache. He poured cereal into a bowl, dumped aspirin on top of it, then poured milk on the whole thing. Standing in his kitchen, he shoveled it in. Above the grinding sound his teeth made, he heard Victoria finish in the shower, heard her pull his towel off the rack. She threw the door open and Wesley saw her naked, toweling herself off, through the steam. He turned his back and finished his bowl, and as Victoria dried her hair, she came in to talk: "Why'd you tell him I was here?" she asked. "What the hell's wrong with you?"

Wesley shrugged. "I'm still half drunk," he said.

"You know how he is," she said.

Wesley nodded in the direction of the bedroom. He said, "So how'd you get him? You give the boy a lap dance or something?"

"Why, Wesley? You jealous?" Victoria asked.

At first Wesley didn't say anything to that. He went to the sink and rinsed his bowl. Then he turned the water off and said, "Allan's a decent man," and that's all he said, and Victoria didn't say another word and got dressed and slammed the door on the way out.

The young man slept through it all, but when Wesley finally heard him wake up, Victoria was long gone. Larry staggered out into the living room, where he found Wesley reading the morning paper.

"Hey, where is she?" he asked.

"She's married, man," Wesley said. "That's where she is."

Wesley wouldn't look at him at first. Larry fidgeted, opening jars filled with scented pieces of paper and picking up magazines and putting them back down. Wesley watched him sideways. He said, "You going to wear that cap all day long?"

Larry reached up to his head and felt the pointed party cap; he grinned and said shit and took it off, setting it on the coffee table.

"Geez," he said.

"Yeah, geez," Wesley echoed, just to have something to say.

"You going to church?" Larry asked.

"Huh uh. You?"

"Huh uh," the young man said. "I don't believe in it. You?"

"No," Wesley said, but he said he went sometimes. "I just like to look at the women all dressed up," he said. "Sometimes I see my kids."

Larry asked him, his own? And Wesley said no, his seventh-graders.

"You a teacher?"

"Yeah," Wesley smiled. "Couldn't you tell?"

"Huh uh," the young man said, grinning.

"Look up there," Wesley said, pointing to a plaque. Larry walked over and read it out loud: "Teacher of the Year. Drexel Street Junior High. Mr. Wesley Adair."

"So what do you think?" Wesley asked.

"School-Wide—that's pretty good."

"They put me up for City-Wide," Wesley said. He held his hands about a yard apart. "I came this close," he said, and the young man laughed heartily and held his hand out to Wesley, and they touched fists and pressed, each man laughing. It was something like a moment. But then the phone rang and Wesley got it. It was Allan again, asking to speak to a "Larry." It was the second time Wesley had spoken to Allan in maybe a year, both times on the same day.

"It's the piper, man," Wesley said, holding the phone out to Larry.

"The piper?"

"Time to pay up," Wesley said.

Larry took the phone and Wesley watched him. He said okay, okay, okay, fine, whatever. When he hung up, Wesley asked him what they talked about, and the young man told him Allan was going to kill him.

"Say that again."

"The guy said he was going to kill me."

Wesley felt his eyebrows raise. "You scared?" he asked.

"Nah, man," Larry said. "I been there before."

Wesley could appreciate swagger—he'd been a marine, after all, and he played some ball too—but he always tried to weigh out just how much was bravery and how much naivete. He looked at the young man and couldn't tell the mix, so he laughed and said, because he didn't know what else to say: "You're an interesting young man, you know that?"

"Sure I know," Larry said, smiling, and they shook hands just like that, beginning in a way that Wesley knew well but advancing to some twists, turns, and hairpins he'd never seen. Wesley started laughing, delighted.

He said, "Give me your phone number. We got to stay in touch."

Larry gave him the number, gladly, and they ate some eggs and toast—the last thing Wesley had left in the house—and then Larry left at one, and Wesley was alone.

The apartment seemed strange to him. He realized it was the first time since he'd moved in that he'd had any company. He looked at the place like a stranger would, saw how bare it looked. He arranged the curtains at the window, trying to let the sunlight in. He took the sheets off the bed and did the wash. He made a note to himself, to go get his car before it got dark—he stuck the note on the bathroom mirror, so he couldn't miss it. He took more aspirin, and then he sat down to prepare his lesson plans for the week. This was how he spent his Sunday afternoons; he liked the routine. He was happy most days if he could reach maybe half the students in his charge—get them to focus. Get them to care. Half was good, he thought. He imagined his classroom, spotting the faces he thought might make it out one day. Two or three of them, he felt like a father to. At church he prayed for them, though he told no one he did such a thing. Maybe he did believe, just a little.

In the next month he and Larry hit the Y and played ball a few times: Larry was good, Wesley thought, and brought a good game of playground ball but moved more like a European player some games, depending on the competition. He could shoot from the perimeter with a graceful stroke that looked like he was born on a ball court, like he'd played college, which one night, at Jimmy's, yes, the young man did confirm. "Just Division III," Larry said, "nothing special."

"State school?" Wesley asked, and the young man said no, a Christian college. Wesley looked at him. "I thought you said you didn't believe," he said, and Larry just said he used to, and that was that.

They drank a lot, Wesley and Larry, and talked a little, just a snatch of conversation here and there, but it wasn't what they said that made the difference, it was just how the two could be together, in one another's presence, and feel like things were right. They saw some old Bogarts at a revival house near the University—they both liked *Key Largo* but Larry said *In a Lonely Place* was way too grim. Once they even met for lunch at a nice restaurant on 53rd Street, at the top of the old bank building. Fish was on special that day (Larry had read somewhere that "oily fish" was healthy). The boy was good company, there was no denying, but always on the run, it seemed. Still, Wesley had his students, he had ball, church on Sundays, running errands for his mom, and he had a friend, of sorts, almost the kind he had longed for, nothing deep, conversationally speaking, but just good, honest camaraderie, proximity, a hand shake or fist press, a quick pass on the court. Then one night Larry let Wesley know he was still seeing a little bit of Victoria. They sat before the mirror at Jimmy's and had been talking to each other's reflection.

"Man, Allan is on to you. I don't think I would, if it was me."

"I'll take my chances," Larry said.

"Why?"

"I think I'm in love," he said.

Wesley got him by the shoulder with one big hand and turned him around on the bar stool: "She could be your mother, man." He said, "She's as old as me."

Larry brushed him off, said he knew that, though he didn't really, Wesley could tell. "You don't understand—I never felt this way before," Larry said.

"Come on, man," Wesley said.

"It's love, Wes."

"It's bullshit, man. She just knows some things girls your age don't, that's all."

Larry gave Wesley a hurt look, and then Victoria walked into the bar, and crossed the room, and stood in between the two of them. She grinned drunkenly.

"How's it goin'?" Wesley said, but only as a matter of courtesy, and Victoria said hey to him, taking Larry by the arm, telling him it was time to go. Wesley watched Larry look into Victoria's eyes. "I'll call you later, Wes," Larry said as he got up and started toward the door with the woman, who glanced back at Wesley and smiled. He watched them walk away. He had a feeling he'd never hear from Larry again.

Back at his place Wesley watched an old movie on late-night TV and drank some whiskey. He hadn't watched a film on TV like that in a long long time. It was called *Picnic*, about a drifter who blew into a small town in Kansas and all the women loved him, from the oldest to the youngest. William Holden played the drifter, and he looked good in his rolled up pants with his shirt half torn—and he could dance, the young man, and move, graceful, but then he stole his best friend's girl, upending lives, the way these things always do. The young man left town the same way he'd ridden in, on a freight, waving from the top of the train as it pulled away and the credits rolled. When the music was done, Wesley saw that his bottle was empty. He woke up in the chair the next morning, the empty bottle between his legs. He turned the TV off. He dragged over to the phone and called in sick, guessing that the kids would be all right.

Wesley's phone rang late some nights, always hang-ups on his machine. Sometimes the caller would wait a few seconds, and lying in his bed, across the apartment, Wesley might hear the sounds of a bar in the background. It could've been Jimmy's, it could've been a lot of places, but he never bothered to check who had called. Whoever it was finally stopped. He went to get some things back from his ex-wife—his CDs, his movies, his books. She left a key out for him one night beneath the door-mat.

Inside his old place Wesley just felt sad. He stood in the hallway. He didn't want to see the bedroom, the upstairs. He stepped down to the basement, where she'd put his old things. He carried out four boxes and left the key where he'd found it, knowing he'd never be back.

Slowly he put his apartment together. He got a new couch, he got a new bed, dragging the old mattress and box springs out to the dumpster. Every now and then he'd venture out to Jimmy's, but mostly the only other place he ever went was school. He showed his kids slides of the Mediterranean, ancient ruins dotted across a blue blue sea. They moved down to Egypt, the pyramids an easy sell. The images always held his kids' attention, and Wesley talked about their history, their construction, the use of slaves to push and drag the stones. The kids wanted to know a lot more about that, and Wesley had the scoop.

On his way home from work one night he saw Larry's car parked outside the Y. He found a parking space on Dorchester and made his way inside to the gym. There was Larry, grabbing a rebound and outletting to a fast little point guard, a guy Wesley had played ball with years before—Larry was so fast he made it to the wing in time to get the bounce-pass for the lay-up, he was that young and that quick. Wesley heard a woman whistling up in the crowd and knew instantly it was Victoria. He made his way up into the stands and sat beside her. She smiled at him briefly but continued to watch the game. Another rebound for Larry, another whistle from Victoria. In the light of the gymnasium, Wesley could see how she'd grown old around her eyes—circles whited out, bags slight but there. Just past her chin, along the jaw line, the skin sagged forward when she bent her head down to check her watch.

"Stop staring, Wesley," she said.

"Sorry," he said.

A whistle blew on the court, a slap foul, side out. Larry ran the ball up the court, form flawless, a dribble between his leg turning out to be a surprise bounce pass to a wing man, who got the easy lay-up.

"He runs pretty hard," Wesley said.

"He sure does," Victoria said.

"How's Allan?"

"Allan is Allan," Victoria said.

"You reach some kind of understanding?"

"More or less," she said, keeping her eyes on the court. "We're going to the bar later, if you're interested."

"You and Allan?"

She looked at him. "Me and Larry," she said.

The game was winding down, just a few more seconds. Larry stood in the center of the key, legs crouched, hands up, defending.

Wesley tapped Victoria's arm with his fist and got up and left the stands, walking back outside to his car. No one was on the street. He drove up Blackstone, took the right on Garfield, drove past the bar, which was quiet and dim. Maybe just one, he thought. He parked just beyond the fire station next door to Jimmy's. He could see the firemen inside playing cards around a table.

Inside Jimmy's he saw Allan sitting in the same old spot, beside the one Wesley used to take back when he was still married. He walked up to it and said hey. Allan looked at him in the mirror.

"Hey, Wesley."

They shook, old school, business, Allan turning toward Wesley slightly, then gesturing to Wesley's old chair, which Wesley took.

"It's me and you," Wesley said.

"Yep," Allan said.

"Long time."

"Yep."

Wesley ordered a drink from a bartender he'd never seen, a pretty blond girl in her twenties, long hair lying across her shoulders.

"Nice, huh?" Allan said as she went to get Wesley his drink.

"If you like them young," Wesley smiled.

She set it down before him. A shot of Jack, his old drink, which Wesley had always sipped. He sipped it, then set it down.

They didn't say anything for a few minutes. Then Allan said, "Victoria still sneaks around with that boy of yours."

"Larry?"

"Yeah."

Wesley nodded. "He's young," Wesley said.

"He'll learn," Allan said.

They got a little bit drunk together, before Wesley could say any of the things on his mind—about Victoria and what really happened or the possibility that she might show up at the bar. Allan had the girl turn the TV to ESPN, which had a soccer match on that they laughed at awhile, neither man really knowing how the game worked. There hadn't been any soccer when they were kids growing up in the city. No one knew what it was back then. Not till somewhere in the Eighties did anyone kick a ball around like that in the park, and then it caught on big.

And then Larry and Victoria stepped into the bar and walked up to Wesley and Allan like it was the most natural thing in the world. Allan had been expecting them, Wesley realized, and Allan was all smiles, a hug for his wife, a slap on the arm for Larry. "Hey, Wes," Larry said, "how you been?" "Fine," Wesley said, "real good," trying to take everything in. He hadn't anticipated this, everybody friendly, or pretending to be, but he tried to roll with it. He wished he hadn't had so much whiskey.

The four of them found a table, and it was Larry, mostly, who went to get their drinks—he had a nervous energy from the game anyway, he said, and he'd won some kind of bet at work, a March Madness thing. Mostly it was Allan Larry spoke to, clearly enjoying their give and take about the DePaul Blue Demons, or maybe it was Marquette, something about zone defense or man to man. Wesley watched as Larry placed his arm on the back of Victoria's chair, his face close to hers as he leaned across to speak to Allan, who was smiling all the while. Then Victoria came around the table to sit with Wesley. She laughed and said, Jesus, those two are thick as fleas. Then she put her hand on Wesley's leg and looked up into his eyes.

He tried to sober up, assess the new terrain, so much like the old terrain, he now realized—treacherous. He found an opening in which he could stand up to leave, gracefully, saying he'd be in touch, but just wanting nothing more than to flee. They all smiled and said something, and Wesley was turning around in the room, heading for the door, passing by tables of students, of Croatian janitors, old Jazz musicians, a table of South Asian men discussing accelerator physics and smashing particles, and then the street, black and wet, a rain having come, and his car just around the corner, clicking his key ring, his car's chirp. Larry found him out on the street, just as Wesley was about to get into his car.

"Hey, Wes!"

Wesley turned. "Yeah, man?"

"Look, I been meaning to tell you this, like bad."

"Well tell it, then."

Larry, swaying just a little on the street, it seemed to Wesley, said, "I'm happy, man." He meant Victoria, Wesley knew.

"You're happy?"

"Yeah!"

Wesley smiled. "You just be happy then. Nothing wrong with that," Wesley said. He shook Larry's hand.

"We're talking marriage, man."

"Marriage, huh?"

"Yeah!"

Larry looked like he might cry, he was so goddam happy.

"Well, good luck with that," Wesley said, retrieving his hand.

"Thanks, Wes. That means something, from you."

Wesley nodded. Then he got into his car, waved, and drove away, down Woodlawn, toward his apartment building, past the liquor store, the hardware store, Kimbark Plaza, to the back of his building. He parked the car in front of the overflowing dumpster— boxes visible, big white bags of bundled trash. He turned off his lights and sat there in the dark. The lot was full. Everyone was home.

ISLAND

It is Sunday night. Usually we sit before our desks on Sunday nights and plan our weeks, I my client list, my wife her various social duties—her clubs, the charities, the attention to those less fortunate, to the up and coming. Sunday nights are usually quiet, but this one turns out not to be. Instead, a woman I have not heard from for seven years—a Mrs. Arnett—calls me on the phone. "There's a problem," she says—no greeting, no asking to speak with me before launching in, which I roll with, no slouch for repartee.

"What problem?"

"It's about your son, Edward," she says, "and my girl."

"Which girl?"

"Barbara," she says. "About your boy and my Barbara."

"I didn't know they were in touch," I say.

She laughs. "It's funny," she says, "how these things tend to repeat themselves—the sins of the father, you know."

"You always had a way with the Bible," I say, thinking of my past infidelities, most of them with her.

"You should come over," she says. "This kind of thing is best discussed in person."

"When?" I say.

"Now" she says. "Now's good."

I cut the connection, no goodbye, a perfect symmetry for such a call. I put on the best damage-control face I can muster and tell my wife, who looks at me like this is my fault, which indirectly, I suppose, it is.

"I knew we hadn't seen the last of that bitch," my wife says.

"That aside," I say, "there's a potential problem here."

"I doubt it's our son's fault," my wife says.

She stands before the fireplace, orange logs roaring behind her, the stone wall containing them, the stone mantle lined with photos of the family. Head shots of me, her, the son in question, another son in Chicago, a self-shot standing in front of a Toulouse-Lautrec, like he's one more gambler at a table—that one, at least, shows a little creativity. Sparks crackle behind her; something shifts on the pile. She's holding the latest issue of *Glamour* in one hand, a glass of Chardonnay in the other.

"It's not like his track record's pristine," I say.

She emits a cruel bark, something she would call a laugh. "He didn't get it from my side," she says. She tips the Chardonnay to her lips and lets her eyes meet the ceiling—you can practically hear the whoosh of the glass as it empties.

"How do you know that? Your father, drunk, speaking of the apple not falling far, told me some pretty interesting stories down through the years."

"My father's dead," she says.

"I'm aware," I say, "because, one, I attended his funeral—brought on by a ripe old age, nothing tragic—and two, to bring it up the way you just did is a non-sequitur."

She sets her glass down and turns to the fire. She starts to cry, or goes through the motions, at least—you never know which with her, and either way, it's a performance.

"Look, I have business," I say, finding my wallet and my keys.

"There's no business like old business," she says, shaking her head, slowly, letting that two-hundred-dollar haircut shimmer in the firelight.

I drive across town. It's the bad side of town I drive for, across the old bridge the city hopes will rot and fall with these people who live out here on it, fall into the deep river, the muddy water, not to be heard from again. The son in question once said the best part about living in Pittsburgh was that if a person ever wanted to drown himself, he had three rivers to choose from. However much a nihilist the little bastard can be, I have to admire his proficiency with numbers, something he did get from me.

I drive, silent, along the island's river road. The smoke stacks sit mute, not used for decades now. I do the mental accounting, wondering how much this little problem will cost me—personally, for one thing, financially for another. Mrs. Arnett worked for me once. It was a long time ago. We got too cozy working late sometimes, and she got me to come out here, to the island, to finish a few reports—a stupid move on my part, one I made many times. My wife was waiting up for me one night, and two weeks later, to the day, Mrs. Arnett was unemployed. Now, as I understand it, she has other arrangements—a wealthy man who lives out in the country, near Ligonier, mails her a check each month; comes by, along this very road, when he can get away from his wife. When I watch the news I see his commercials, yet another example of how small a world it is for those of us who cheat, a finite number, apparently, of willing women but a large number of willing men. On the screen he calls himself the ATV King, sells something called the "four-wheeled monster," for ten-year-old boys out there in the Laurel Highlands to kill themselves upon. His smiling wife stands beside him in the most recent spot, and his boy, decked out in a crash helmet and elbow and knee pads, runs a monster ATV straight up a hillside, disappearing like a deer into the brush. The camera cuts to the smiling mother, who looks at the camera and says she wouldn't let her son ride something that wasn't safe, and then it cuts back to the King, who's pointing at the camera talking about slashed prices and getting "the most ATV value for your American dollar." He's not a bad man, I suppose. Lord knows what my own commercials would look like, were I to feel the need.

The road narrows and then comes to a complete stop. Drive another twenty feet and you drive into the river. This is where she lives, at the end of the island, the one bridge the only way in, and out. I pull the car up to the garage that her apartment sits upon.

The garage is dark for the night; cars hulk inside, through the glass, in the shadows made by the streetlight. The door off to the side, at the bottom of her stairs, is unlocked—the way it used to be. I start up the stairs, pulling shut the door; it clicks behind me like a gun cock. The second door is open at the top of the stairs—also like it used to be. Mrs. Arnett is sitting on her couch, dressed in a short bathrobe, nothing on beneath it, it seems. This is not necessarily a come-on: it's always too warm inside her apartment, she used to say. She always said she was warm-blooded—too warm-blooded for anyone's good. She liked to say she could dress exactly like she wants in her own place, that no one could tell her different. It's dim inside that place. The windows are open and the breeze that comes off the river blows her thin curtains full, like sails.

"Come in, Mr. Brock," she says, smiling. She gestures to a chair across from the couch. *Masterpiece Theatre* is on and I had forgotten that she considers herself some kind of connoisseur of high art—or what she considers high art. Myself, I no longer give a shit about the distinction, but she did, probably still does.

"Five years," she says.

"Seven," I correct, and again she smiles. "I shave a few myself sometimes," I say. "But seriously, my wife's waiting for me down in the car, so let's make this quick."

"Her? Here? Please."

"In spirit," I say, and she smirks.

"I just need ten minutes of your time," she says, "seriously," and she tells me she has a story to tell.

"About my boy?" I say, and she nods.

"Smoke?" she asks, gesturing to the table beside her, the opened pack, the Zippo lighter, the dead cigarettes in her plastic ashtray. The whole place smells like stale smoke. "I quit," I say, and she smiles like that's exactly what she expected to hear.

"A bunch of the kids were out on the mountain the other night," she says, "at the drive-in restaurant out by the big incline." I nod. "And your boy happened to be there sitting in his Bronco, looking sweet, maybe a little drunk already, according to my Barbara. He was two cars over from hers, and he sees her, recognizes her, calls out, says, 'Hey, your name is Barbara, right?' My little girl, so sweet and untouched, she says, 'Yes, yes my name is Barbara,' and he tells her who he is and she says, 'I know, my mother used to work for your father,' and your boy says, 'I know, and when we were little,' he says, 'we used to play together.'"

Mrs. Arnett gets up and walks across the room, shuts off the TV. "It's such a nuisance sometimes," she says. She's a tall woman—beats my wife, who's not short, by three inches. She's put on weight, a little heft now to that stomach, down low. She sees me looking, turns sideways a little as she walks back. She's got a tan from somewhere, maybe from lying out on her rooftop, the one off to the side of her bedroom. Maybe from a tanning booth in a cheap salon.

"That's a nice coat," she says, sitting back down.

"It was a birthday gift," I say.

"From the little woman," she says. Then she looks at me, disgusted. There is a bag of chips in the floor beside her chair, unopened. She reaches down and tears the top off it, starts to crunch, talking as she chews. "So your boy continues to drink," she says. "Want one?" She holds out the bag. I shake my head. "He continues to drink," she goes on, and I can see her jaw muscles working over those chips, chewing, grinding. "He continues to drink," she says, "and he gets drunk. He steps out of his Bronco and walks over to my Barbara and he says, 'Babe, how'd you like to fuck?'"

I must look surprised, which seems to please her.

"That's what he says," Mrs. Arnett says. "Your boy says to my little Barbara, 'Babe, how'd you like to fuck?'" She draws out the fuck, says it quizzically. She squeezes the bag of chips in her big fist and I can hear them breaking. She leans forward.

"Your boy," she says to me, still leaning forward, "asks my little girl, if she'd like to F-U-C-K. Now, you tell me, Mr. Brock, where he got an attitude like that. I mean," she says, "you tell me, why he thinks that a hoity-toity college sonofabitch like himself can ask such a thing of a sweet, nice little somebody like my Barbara."

"I don't know why he'd say such a thing," I say. "How was she dressed that night?"

Her eyes narrow. "What does how she's dressed have to do with it?" she says.

"I don't know," I say. "Was she, for example, dressed in a robe that was maybe too short for her?"

Mrs. Arnett draws her head back a little, like a bird on alert in a tree-top.

"Because if she was," I say, "I would have to say that it might be possible that she was hoping some hoity-toity sonofabitch might just ask such a thing."

"No woman ever asks for such a thing, Mr. Brock," she says. "Contrary to what men your age might think, women never ask for it."

The comment about age hurts, but I try not to wince; besides, I think she's wrong, at least partly—all men of all ages are all pig a hundred percent of the time, and if they say they're not, it's because they're trying to impress somebody, like a woman in a hotel bar from a Seven Sisters college (assuming she's straight), or like the Sexual Harassment Officer of a half-baked corporation out in LA.

She reaches into the bag for more chips, but they're all broken now, and she can fish out only small bits and crumbs. "Shit," she says, and flings them across the room, spraying me and the TV screen with crumbled chips.

"So is there more to the story?" I say, brushing chip bits off my pant legs, my coat. "I don't have much longer."

"Yes, there's more," Mrs. Arnett says. And she tells me the rest in a rush: He, my boy, chases Barbara down the mountain road in the car. Barbara has to run red lights, go through stop signs without stopping: two big headlights from a four-wheel drive in her rearview, blinding her. She has to drive so fast that she bottoms out over a pothole, breaking off her muffler—she sees it slide across the highway, the Bronco behind her swerving, but then straightening, following. Barbara drives all the way home with no muffler—down the Parkway, across the bridge, along the river road—and jumps out of the car and throws the lock at the bottom of the stairs, and just as she does so, my boy bounds up to the door like a madman and starts twisting the knob. He presses his mouth and nose up against the glass obscenely and slobbers on it and screams like a banshee. Barbara sits at the bottom of the stairs and cries. The men are working downstairs late in the car shop, though, and they come outside with tire-irons and chains and chase him off.

"And where were you at the time?" I ask.

She looks at me: "Away," she says, and I flash on the verdant hillsides of Ligonier and her and the ATV King crisscrossing its bounty on one of his products. "His spit's still on the window down there, if you want to look," she continues. "His mouth-prints too. The whole window's smeary, like the inside of a car window where a baby's been wiping its hands along."

"So you want me to pay for the muffler," I say.

"It would be nice," she says, "if you could pay. I could ask him," she says, meaning the King, "but it wouldn't be right. It might interest you to know that I called your son and asked him to pay. I was trying to leave you out of this. He said I should call you anyway."

"I'll talk to him myself," I say. "I'll get back to you."

"When?" she says, a little angry, maybe, or maybe desperate—something.

"Immediately," I say, and I can see her smirk to herself.

"Immediately is good," she says. Then her expression softens, the business part done for now. "Remember how it was?" she asks, and I do but I don't want to admit it—being here brings it back, all of it, especially the bad.

"No," I say, "I don't remember." She stands up then, in that short little robe she's wearing, to shake my hand—formally, like you do in an office. I stand and reach out, and I hear, just around the corner, the sound of someone walking down the hall. It is Barbara who rounds the corner, and she is exactly the image of her mother, only wide-eyed when she sees us. She has just stepped out of the shower and is wrapped in a towel, her black hair dripping wet. When I register inside her head, she turns quickly and says, "Excuse me, I'm sorry, I didn't know ..." Her voice trails down the hallway, back to where the bedrooms are.

"She's in school to be a secretary," Mrs. Arnett tells me.

"I'll call you," I say.

"I know you will," she says.

I pause as I pull shut the door at the bottom of the stairs. I can't bring myself to turn and study the windowpane, though I can imagine my son's lips upon it, his tongue. In the car I phone my wife, tell her the story and get a few pregnant pauses. As I drive across town, back toward the house, still on the phone, she says she doesn't believe any of it, that our boy wouldn't do any of those things. I tell her I have to talk to our son regardless, that I need to hear his side. I pull into our driveway, and from the car I turn on the floodlights and open the garage door: she is standing there with the bank card, holding it like in a relay. It's just a way of saving a little money not to carry it around, that's all, though more than once not having it has been a nuisance. I can't see her eyes, the way she's standing in the light; her hair is back-lit, a little like a Romero film. I tell her I'll be home when all this is settled, and then I watch her walk back inside on her heels—she is fast, precise, rhythmic: her heels slash across the floor like pickaxes.

Across town, past the park, past the college, I buzz my son's apartment. As I step inside Edward tells me he's surprised to see me. His place is not quite a dormitory room, but is instead something the college calls a student condo. He has one roommate, who's always away for the weekend, so it's just the two of us.

He invites me to sit and then sits across from me, his chair turned around, its back facing me, his legs splayed by the back. He's majoring in business economics. He's told me he wants to live in Connecticut one day and work in Manhattan. He's told me he wants to run a whole corporation, not just a small office. I think all this unlikely. I think he will work for me and marry a nice girl and live in Shadyside and have two children, like we did. My younger son, Jake, who favors his mother, is a different story. His life I can't begin to predict, but Edward, his life I know.

I tell him Mrs. Arnett's story and he hedges. He says he remembers something about seeing Barbara Arnett the other night, but he doesn't remember chasing her in his Bronco, and he certainly doesn't remember pressing his face up against the glass in their doorway. He smiles engagingly all the while that he is refuting. I ask him if the story is possibly true, and he says anything is possible, and then he smiles again.

I take out my phone and call Mrs. Arnett, my fingers easily remembering the sequence. She tells me she knew I'd call back, that she is waiting for me. She is leering into the phone as she says it—I know her voice, its inflections, and how they match her face. I tell her I'll bring the money and I break the connection before she can respond.

"You shouldn't take advantage of a girl like that," I say to my son. I say it's not right, that they're desperate for attention from a boy like him. He's wearing a baseball cap backward on his head, his shirt hangs out, his shorts hang down to his knees. He's wearing shoes so loud that in my day only people living in the Hill District would have worn them.

"Gosh, Dad," he says. "That's sage advice, the kind that sounds like it comes from experience—not that I'm implying anything, mind you." He smiles. "But look, I'm really beat, okay, so I'm going to bed. Just see yourself out, okay?" He salutes and turns down the hall. "Oh," he says, "about Barbara Arnett? You know, I knew she was a little whore when we were kids together. Did you know that?" His back is to me down at the end of the hallway, where he stands before his door. "You could just tell. Jake knew it too. In fact, I'm pretty sure those two had at it, once, maybe twice, so you might want to drop in on him, too, to see what he has to say about this little piece of business." He tells me to have a nice evening and his bedroom door closes, clicking nicely into place. Outside it has begun to mist. My glasses fog up in the darkness.

I stop at a drive-through cash machine in downtown Pittsburgh and get five-hundred dollars, the limit. In my rearview, as the machine grinds out the money, I watch a homeless man pass behind my car. He looks inside at me and thinks better of it, passes on, looking for someone else to hit up. Five hundred should be enough for the muffler, and for the window at the foot of her stairs. I get my emergency card out of the glove, punch in a different account, get five hundred more, figuring that that'll be enough to keep her from calling me again. Outside her place I see his Escalade parked by the side of the garage, partly hidden by the boughs of a pine tree. On its front plate is a sign that says I Heart Ligonier. Her door is locked.

I search in the darkness for a rock, a brick, finding a discarded piece of tailpipe from the repair shop. I rubberband the bills to the pipe, then shove it through her windowpane, cutting the top of my hand. The window shatters satisfactorily, the dried spittle and lip-smears falling away with the glass. The pipe clangs down onto the floor. A light goes on upstairs, and then another, down at the far end of the apartment. Footsteps come heavily down the stairs—they could be hers or that Barbara's, maybe his, I can't be sure. "Don't cut your feet," I say through the window into the stairwell. She flicks her lighter, bending down in the darkness, among the glass, searching. I see her crouched, naked. I hear the twang of the rubber band, the sound of paper snapping ten times in her hands.

"Is that enough?" I ask, and I hear her flick shut the lighter. "Yes," Mrs. Arnett says, "it's enough."

"It's pennies," I say.

"It's principle," she says.

"His car," I say, nodding toward the tree.

"His wife's away," she says. "I didn't know."

As I pass along the dying bridge I wish that now would be the time it chooses to collapse, dumping me into the dirty water, washing my car along the Ohio into the Mississippi into the Gulf. Downtown I pull the car over to the edge of the Parkway. I tie a white cloth to the antenna and walk down over the hill and see it in all its stink, the mighty Mon. I bend down to it and stick my bloody hand in, letting the current carry the mess away—down, eventually, to her little island. It's cold, the water. Very cold.

ABANDON

*A*male child grows up in a house of plenty. His father runs a
successful paper business and sells his stock to phone companies
and newspapers all over Western Pennsylvania. The family lives in
Squirrel Hill and the office is downtown and the father works late
often because he is cheating on his wife. The man occasionally takes
the boy with him on his runs. The boy is sworn to secrecy and sits in
the woman's living room with a girl his age while his father attends to
his, and his employee's, needs.

One day the boy wanders the woman's home and sees his father
behind her as she leans against her washing machine, his hands
around her neck, the woman gasping for air as she tries to speak. She
is naked to the waist, her skirt bunched around her middle.

Shortly afterward, the boy starts walking in his sleep.

He breaks things at first, as he wanders the house in the early
hours of the morning. He pees sometimes in the hallway. He leaves
the windows open in the coldest weather. Then he goes to his bedroom
and lies in bed the rest of the night. By the time he wakes up, the mess
is always gone. He is never made any the wiser. He'll grow out of it,
the family doctor says.

When the cat is found rigid one morning on the kitchen floor,
its neck broken, no one says a thing to the boy except that the cat has
gone away to live with distant cousins.

Sometimes in his mind he sees these nocturnal wanderings as
they unfold as dreams. More often he operates in an oblivious state,
unaware and unregistering, though occasionally, at odd moments in

the daytime, bits and pieces come back. The sound of glass breaking, the sudden cold smell of the out of doors, a flash of yellow fur and sharp, hissing teeth.

When he gets old enough, somewhere into puberty, he starts to drink and becomes what some would call a binge drinker, but only when the memories come too close.

He becomes a star student in high school and later earns a B.S. in finance at C.M.U. He dates a girl who cheats on him repeatedly and when he walks in on her in the act with a random college boy his mind will not allow him to register the thing he sees.

He graduates with honors and, through family connections, acquires a job in the city of Chicago. His parents hope the nightwalking is behind him and that his drinking won't get too bad. They help him find a modest apartment and give him only start-up funds, believing a young man in a new city must make it on his own. He misses a lot when he interacts with others, but he's used to social encounters that don't quite make sense. He gives himself over to this world with a kind of abandon, taking in as much as he can, hoping that one day everything will click.

Rather than take a seat he stood in the vestibule because he enjoyed the rocking of the train, which rode through Hyde Park, Kenwood, along Lake Michigan toward downtown. The neighborhoods changed, from posh to ghetto to something in between. And then a quick clip through the maze-like station, past lunch counter, flower shop, shoeshines, panhandlers, the stairs and streets teeming.

His beacon the Sears Tower, he walked toward its height, arrived at his desk with steep coffee and warm doughnut, murmured greetings to co-workers and his boss. High fives, thumbs up, slaps from behind. Printouts from the night before laid down and he pored over them fruitfully, deep focus his forte, something of a gift. He could discern patterns in rune-like graphics and scatterplots no one else could see. Probability was a number to him, a thing of the eye, no figment. Buy this, he would say; sell that; keep an ear to the stone.

Evenings, he studied names of places and people who mattered: buildings, architects, CEOs (the Wrigleys, Sullivans, and Burnetts). He stopped by the Art Institute one Saturday each month, seating himself before a Caillebotte one visit (*Paris on a Rainy Day*), a Van Gogh the next (*The Bedroom*). He raced through handbooks on urban fancies like avant-garde and genre film, alternative music and postwar Jazz, California wine and foreign beers. He scoured inky underground newspapers to find twenty-something scenes: neighborhood wines and cheese; alt bands in Lower Loop lofts; U.S. premieres of small German films by Kluge, Speiker, or Straub.

He would open a Chardonnay and sip, blacking the stem of the wine glass with his fingers. He would scrub his nails with a potent soap and bristly, painful brush. He would discover that even fine wine caused his stomach to twist, some chemical in the grape that triggered painful gastric contortions. He would forgo wine when his girl came to visit—not unless he wanted to be doubled over on the carpet at midnight, grunting, anguished, and ashamed.

"The man I marry has got to have big bucks," his fiancee said to him. "I mean really big, you got me?"

He got her. He was pretty sure he didn't deserve her, but there she was, a Communication major back home. Long hair, dark eyes, tasteful style, kind of Asian. They had met in a Humanities course and she loved *King Lear* best and he joked that he himself would've made a great fool. She liked that; she laughed. She cooked for him and made love to him that same night, and that was that. They found a place and he filled her shelves and she kept her friends and he let his go, one by one. The day before he left town for Chicago he gave her the rock—a beacon, a warning, a small craft advisory. She slipped it on. "Any port in a storm," she said.

The memories came back sometimes in dreams. Walking into the apartment he shared with her and sitting patiently on the couch while she toiled away in the back room with a friend. The boy, his age, finally walks out. "She doesn't love you," he says. "She never really has." He looks at her as she stands behind the boy, her arms around his waist. He waits for a long time—waits for him to laugh, or her to laugh, both. The laughter never comes, and the boy leaves and the two who remain sit across the room from each other, mute.

At work they began to call him the Wiz, his facility with software growing more advanced by the month. He coded subroutines he bootstrapped onto statistical procedures, his co-workers astounded by his predictions, both potent and true.

He displayed a picture of his girl, one that sat on his desk in a finite, knowable space. It humanized him, allowed others to feel like there was more to him than incredible proficiency and a work ethic second to none.

He walked to the train through a snowy, freezing Loop and fell asleep after eating Lean Cuisine, dreaming of the day he would be wed.

Some nights he awoke in a panic, bolt upright, grasping at a phantom image of his girl. Other nights he dreamed he followed her down a shadowy street. One night he found himself in a cabaret, a woman's scarf in his hand, a drag queen in white singing Mariah Carey on the stage.

"How long have I been here?"

"What?"

"When did I get here?"

The bartender looked at him. "Midnight," he said.

He played it cool; this sort of thing happened. Get your bearings, he thought—city, street, distance from home. Name the people you know, the place that you work, the day that this is.

"You okay?" the bartender asked.

"Sure," he said. "You?"

"I'm not the one with big saucer eyes, buddy. Just trying to help out."

"You Are My Hero" the song being sung and the saunter for the door past queers a million and the long walk home, breathing deep, seeing the bank clock and trying to calculate lost time. Snow falling, jacket too thin, home in bed and telling yourself to forget it, forget it, you'll be just fine. The city was blanketed in snow and the mayor didn't know what to do. No one had been to work for two days. No trains. No buses. Only white all around.

The drag queen lived down the hall from his apartment. Forty. Maybe forty-five. Fairly thin. One evening she spoke to him on the elevator.

"I wish you wouldn't come by tonight," she said.

"Excuse me?"

He was holding the door to the elevator, so she could exit first.

"Not tonight," she said. "I have guests."

"Do we know each other?" he asked.

"You're a riot," she said, squeezing his arm, walking off the elevator in her tight white dress.

He let the door close and stood there, his mind going blank. At the pizza shop he ordered a large sausage and mushroom. February was a monster that blew hard and fast. You needed good boots, a warm coat, hot food. At work that day he had accomplished what others had thought was impossible, though to him the signs had been obvious. He had made his firm a cool million in ten minutes, the other analysts looking at him with gimlet eyes. "The bonus period has passed," his boss had said, "but you'll see it in your raise."

Back in his building on his floor he passed the drag queen's apartment—Latin music welled but his mind was focused on pulling off his coat, taking off his boots, digging in. Pizza in Chicago was better than back home, the huge disk cut into small squares, a city scene by Giacometti. Entire blocks disappeared as he drifted into a stupor, hearing a voice that told the following story: "There was this one guy in particular, I just hated the bastard. So smug. He thought I didn't know, and I didn't, in a way, but part of me did.

"He would bicycle sometimes in Schenley Park in the early morning hours and I would follow along, slowly, far behind in my car. I figured out his pattern—what time he rode that bike, how he dressed, who else was around at that hour. Like clockwork.

"So at 2:21 A.M. on a Tuesday in May, in a blind curve in the park, nobody else in sight, I butted his bike tire from behind and watched that bastard's bicycle veer off the road and jet down the hill toward a crop of rocks. Fucker was in a body cast in Allegheny General all that summer. She wasn't getting any dick those days from him, that's for damn sure."

When spring came to Chicago he walked the streets. He passed brownstones. Passed elaborate houses. A mansion. A row of public housing. One evening he found himself in a rundown section, and on the roof of a particular wood-frame—the roof above a small stoop—sat a young black man and a fleshy blond woman, side by side. "Hey! Baryshnikov!" the blond called out—he had just tripped on a piece of broken sidewalk—"What's your name?" and he told her his name was Jake, Jake Brock.

Inside their place, Jake was handed a beer. He chatted with the black guy and white girl, Russell and Alex, respectively. It was Alex's place, one she shared with a roommate, Jeannette, who waitressed a bar down the street. When Alex got up to retrieve three more beers, Russell slid down beside him on the couch and whispered: "She hot, man. She like it. Just get her drunk, you know?"

Jake was dumbstruck. He had thought that despite the waitress-girlfriend story, Russell and Alex were surely intimate.

"What?"

"She do it, man. She like it."

Alex stepped into the room, smiling.

"What?" she said.

Russell smiled but said nothing. They drank their beers. They talked modern art, the cost of produce, whether Hyde Park or Lincoln Park was a better place to live. Then they were off down the street in the dusk, streetlights buzzing on. They were walking to a bar, Jake barely catching things that Alex, the girl, and Russell, the guy, were saying. Something about Jeannette and dollar drinks.

"Purple Jesus?" Alex said as they passed a jive joint with dollar-drink recipes plastered on the door. "I never heard of that. I just think Jim Jones when I hear someone mention Kool-Aid, don't you?"

Then he was sitting at a booth with them saying he was from Pittsburgh. He could hear his own voice somehow, syncopated, and he realized he was drunk. He seemed to be getting along better with Alex, who sat beside him running her hand along his arm, and Russell, who was telling a roundabout joke. Jake laughed when Alex laughed.

A bar maid came over. Jeannette. Brown hair, chic glasses, no smile—she was too busy to smile, she said. She shook Jake's hand and went back to the bar and got a tray of drinks, which she carried to the next room. Alex moved to the other side of the table.

"Is it something I said?"

"No," Alex shouted above Dire Straits. "I just want a better look at you."

Russell said, "Look like a good time to give you two a moment." Alex smiled and let him out, and Russell stood up, gave Jake a peace symbol, and walked away.

Later, Jake would remember chuckling at Russell's timely exit. Would remember how he could see, just over Alex's shoulder, two white guys slam Russell against the wall by the jukebox, lay a fist into his ear. Remember Alex's blond head blotting out the kicking legs and fallen man, who was dragged into the bathroom, her innocent mouth asking about the gin and tonic back at his apartment.

"My apartment?" he would remember saying.

"Is that an invitation?" she had said.

He wanted to speak about something that mattered—maybe what had just happened by the men's room, or maybe his fiancee back home—but he had blanked on those already, so all he said was yeah, it was.

"Let me just tell Russell and Jeannette where I'm going," Alex shouted above the jukebox, and Jake said don't worry about them, seriously, they'll figure it out. "Someone's eager," she said, smiling. Another blackout and they were a few blocks from his apartment on foot. "This way," Alex, who knew the right combination of streets, said.

"How well do you know Russell?" Jake asked.

"Pretty well," Alex said. "We grew up together."

"Around here?"

"No," Alex said. "Downstate. Small town."

"You have black people in small towns in Illinois?"

"Yeah," Alex said. "Don't you, in Pennsylvania?"

They were standing inside his apartment and he was holding a drink.

She held her glass out to his. "Cheers," she said, and they drank, and he remembered her smiling and reaching out to touch his arm.

The next morning his phone was ringing, his hand grasping, his fiancee saying something about coming out to see him.

"What's that?" he said. His head hurt. He was half drunk and half asleep. "You're coming out?" Yes, she said, she was coming out. She told him, flatly, that she was landing at O'Hare the next weekend.

Beside the phone he saw a note from Alex: "I had a good time," it said. "Please come look for me again." She had signed her name "Alexandria," like the city in Egypt.

He saw her at the gate. She had cut her hair severely, but otherwise she looked the same. She had one small bag, which she insisted that she carry herself.

She only let him kiss her cheek, and on the way to his place, sitting on the hard plastic seat of the train, she let him know she was marrying someone else. The image of a body cast flitted through his mind as she was saying she felt like she owed him this trip out, to tell him to his face. She slipped the ring into his palm. "You're the dumbest genius I ever knew," she said.

She slept on the floor beside his bed. In the morning he awoke to see her standing by his desk, reading Alex's note, which he'd left out. He saw her shake her head, heard her snort, chuckle, choke—something. By the time she turned to look at him, his eyes were closed. He listened to her call a cab and decided the best thing was to sleep through her leaving. When he woke up later that day, he found the trash full of every glass he owned, every one in pieces. He could see the ring, tiny, at the bottom of the heap. He quietly bundled it, carefully carried it down the hall to the trash chute—he listened to it drop and then made his way to the supermarket and bought new glasses boxed up something like a six-pack.

He still had work; he was good at that, making charts and graphs, plotting regression curves and locating the best point at which to push a market, or back down, or buy or sell or hold. His annual eval was the best the boss had ever given to someone only twenty-two.

"Goddam, Jake," his boss said at lunch. "I've never seen anyone good as you." His boss chewed a piece of thick steak and looked at him—a long look indeed.

At midnight the drag queen knocked on his apartment door. Jake stood on the other side, listening.

"I know you're there," she said. "I just wanted to be the first to wish you a happy birthday."

Jake's clock read 12:01.

The next morning outside his door he found a bottle of expensive wine, a black bow-tie around its neck.

Five weeks to the day his fiancee had left his life forever, Jake went out in search of Alex. He walked the streets for hours but could not find the one she lived on—the houses looked wrong, and then he was in the ghetto, and white people drove past in cars and shouted to him not to walk any farther. He stood among ruins. He turned and started systematically to go up and down the streets, but nothing looked quite right. He hadn't caught the street name, hadn't even caught her last name. Her note was in his pocket.

At sunset he managed to find the pub. When he stepped inside, he realized it had been redone—new paint, new booths, new lights. He walked to the bar and asked the bartender if he knew a girl named Alex and a black guy named Russell.

"You a cop?" the bartender, cleaning a pair of beer glasses on brushes in a sink, asked.

"What? No, I'm not a cop. I'm just looking for this girl."

A man at the end of the bar stared at Jake. The bartender washed another pair of beer glasses and hung them to dry on a pair of angled posts.

Then the bartender came over. He said, "A guy named Russell was killed in here a month ago. The owners lost their license. I bought the place and just opened. I don't know anything about that, all right? Now, do you want a drink, or do you want to leave?"

Jake didn't know what to say. Finally, he said he was sorry and left. Out on the sidewalk the wind was blowing hard, the way it did at dusk. A bank clock showed a temperature of 39 degrees. He hadn't brought his coat. He wasn't sure which way home was. He buttoned the top button of his button-down and pulled it as far up his neck as it would go. He stepped out into the street, which was quiet even for a Sunday, and craned his neck to see if he could see the top of his apartment building. He thought he saw it, finally, to the east, and that's the direction he headed, hands in his pockets, crumpling up the note.

THE IT BOY

It is 4:30 on a Sunday afternoon but already the night is coming on—the sky is darker, cloudier, taking on the orange hue of the Chicago streetlights. On a day like today, with the good Lord in his absence, you have to take stock of yourself, your situation, so here's what I tell myself as my tennis shoes grind out waffle prints in the snow: I am tall, taller than anyone else on the street in February. I am blond-haired and blue-eyed and fair of skin. I am thin, the most desirable whore in Hyde Park. Hell, in the whole South Side. There's only one Joe Smith, I tell myself, and when I tell myself that, I know it isn't so. There are a hundred of me, a thousand— enough Joe Smiths to go around. Enough Joe Smiths to fill up a booth at that Taste of Chicago thing in summer in Grant Park. You can try the blond Joe Smith, the Hispanic Joe Smith, the Negro. Go on, have a taste.

I swagger when I walk but I have a rhythm—not like clumsy-ass white guys who look like gorillas when they try to walk tough. They make me laugh, all the fat little Slavs, afraid some black guy will kick their ass just for being white. Two Serbs pass by on the sidewalk, the children of immigrants, leather jackets and bandanas for caps, a baseball bat in hand and it's not like there's any green diamond of summer to take that bat out to; it's for protection, not too obvious and not too scared a move, but hey, it's a move, at least. They look at me but take me for some kind of Hitler Youth, that hair of mine, no kind of queer, nobody who needs to have his brains flattened out into pierogies, not today anyway, and so I pass myself off for a straight boy and laugh myself all the way down to the Cove, this bar where I first met Ivan, a man I keep meeting almost every day.

But there's no one there, no one worth talking to, not yet—a few old drunks line the bar, men so far past their primes they wouldn't be able to feel it, much less get their tall towers ready. The Bulls are on TV, the drunks glued to the motion. No Michael, no Scottie, no Dennis, just five guys in red uniforms who dish a ball off to no one who wants to shoot. The game's enough to keep the sober ones home still, snack treats on the table, real family adventure. I walk out to the water, watch it knock against slabs at the foot of the path. There's a mist, a spray, plumes that rise thirty feet in the air. One crazy-ass jogger runs by, hooded; he picks up speed when he sees me, and then he's gone and no life is anywhere. It's like this movie I saw once where Vincent Price is the one person left alive after this big plague, *The Last Man on Earth*. In the Men's Room I see they took the doors off the stalls, something that's never done in Women's Rooms. Not that any respectable woman would be caught dead inside of one anyway, except maybe at DisneyLand, or some wacko Christian theme park.

Coming back I hang out by the restaurant just across from the park. I take a couple of walking passes by the door, ignore the valet, who's too cold to give a shit about me, and finally one guy comes out who gives me the eye—forty, maybe forty-five. Tall and trim and well dressed. He raises his chin my way, and I raise mine back and then follow him to his car, a Lincoln Towncar, meaning he has money, of course, but no taste in cars. He pops his lock on the passenger door and I crawl inside.

So what's a guy with a car nice as this doing having dinner alone? I ask him, and he tells me he doesn't want to hear my voice, so I go quiet and wait for his next move. His hands are on the steering wheel and then I see the wedding band. He stares straight ahead in the night, looking out onto the almost empty parking lot and the few cars whizzing by on Lake Shore Drive. He's wearing a nice suit, looking like he made it to church today. He takes a twenty dollar bill from his wallet, which he keeps tucked inside the breast pocket of his suit. He passes me the twenty without looking my way, and then he undoes his wool pants and pulls them down along his hips. His tall tower is ready. I guess he took it easy inside that restaurant on the vodka and tonics, but Monday is a work day, of course, and he looks like the type who tries to get a fresh start on the week by making Sunday a day of rest. It's cold inside the car, the windows beginning to fog up.

He starts the car and the heat blasts out from the vents. The windows unfog quickly, like magic. I warm my hands by a vent, making a little laugh as I do so but trying not to speak any more words, trying to keep the customer happy. He keeps his hands on the steering wheel, hits the horn accidentally when he finds his peak. I try not to imagine the doorman looking our way, not right then, when I'm finishing. I ride with it, not pointing out the rich man's foibles, thinking about the eye of the needle in the old Bible story.

The first guy who ever paid me was named Frank. He wasn't rich, but he was from the suburbs. A lot of them are, they like to pick you up in the city and drive you out to their little neighborhoods. But don't get me started on suburbs, how I feel about them, how they shouldn't even exist, these in-between places. I was just off the bus, had stowed my gear at the Greyhound station and was walking downtown Chicago since two in the morning. It was cold and rainy. I walked up and down the side streets and the main streets, seeing the big museum on Michigan Avenue and making a note of it, seeing the Tribune Building, the big Picasso statue at Daley Plaza. It was a big city but it didn't scare me, almost no one on the streets. I kept looking up into the fog, lit up and twinkling, trying to imagine what the tops of the buildings looked like. It was like canyons down there where I was, like big tall mountains had sprouted up all around me, sheer face, nothing you could rock-climb. I kept criss-crossing State Street, that one Sinatra sings about in his song about the city.

The rain picks up, so I step into a diner, where inside is a counter with a woman. She comes up to me, sees me, wonders what I'm doing there sitting among the drunks and vagrants. What can I get for you, sweetie? she asks.

Coffee, I say.

Come again? she says.

Coffee, I say—a couple of winos staring at me now. She laughs, asks me where I'm from, says I must be from down South with that accent, and I say yeah, I am, around Memphis.

Sure sweetie, she says to me. Wherever.

She pours me a cup, a good scalding one and I sip it slowly, take the place in and realize I must sound like a hayseed. I look at myself in the mirror behind the counter, see that I don't look like a hayseed, at least, looking the way street toughs look in newspaper photos, at least that's what I was shooting for.

I sip my coffee and listen closely to the way the winos around me are talking, taking in their accents, trying to separate slurred speech from real. Every time they say the word car they sound like pirates, like that aar, aar, aar sound Bluto makes in Popeye cartoons. But the waitress, she keeps her eye on me, not because she thinks I'll steal an ashtray or anything, but just because, I can tell, she's worried. Winos leave the counter and drunks filter in off the street, taking their place.

She's a full-figured gal but not too bad, a Gena Rowlands thing going on at the hips and in the face, bleached blond. She doles out more coffee up and down the bar, eighty-sixes one old black man who propositions her, picks up the phone and punches 9-1-1 and the old guy is out the door, not seeing her hold her finger down on the cradle button all the while. She laughs and says he won't be back. A group of cheesy accountants down at the end of the bar get up very quietly, their all-nighter for the boss brought to an end once they pay their bill. One of them looks at me and then looks again, like he wants to say something, or wants me to.

I lay two singles on the counter and get up to leave; she comes over and gets my cup, saucer, spoon and singles in one motion, asks me where I'm going. Out there, I say to her. She stands there holding my things, says, It'll be daylight in about an hour, if you want to wait out the night in here. She's looking at me—at my wet hair and jacket and bumpkin ways. She's a very nice lady, I can tell—not too nice, but just good, sincerely good. That's nice of you, ma'am, I say.

Down the counter a couple of men are calling out for more coffee. You know they have YMCAs all over the city, she says, still holding my cup and saucer.

I know, I say. I read all about it before I came here.

She smiles. You can't learn everything in books, she says.

I'll be all right, I say, and I turn and walk out the door because I have to, because becoming a bus boy in an all night diner is not the kind of thing I had in mind, although it's not like she was offering. But you can see these things coming sometimes. Outside on the street the accountants are long gone.

Downtown one block the elevated train comes clicking down the tracks thirty feet above my head, sparks dropping from the rails, falling down the girder-sides and snapping on the pavement. I walk out into the street and get right beneath the El and watch it roar by above me, gawking like a rube at its underside, sparks falling like July 4th until it disappears behind the buildings. A cab comes up behind me and honks, the driver yelling something. I walk up and down a few more sidewalks, see that the woman had her timing right, that the daylight, such as it is in so grey a place, is about to come—there's a brightening to the sky above the lake, just a little. I head for State Street again, this big wide thing they've cobbled all over, almost no street at all but a lot of sidewalk, for people traffic, it looks like. Some cleaning women are at the bus stop. A newspaper stand is opening, the man setting out his Tribunes and Sun Times. I walk up to him. You get anything from down South? I say. He looks at me. Up early, huh? he says. I say yeah. Just the *Constitution*, he says, out of Atlanta. It'll be here in about an hour. I thank the man.

I wander down State and suddenly there's one of those microbursts of rain, just boom, it hits from out of nowhere. I run up under the door-facing at a store called Carson-Pirie, fluted architecture all around me, some wrought iron stuff they've let turn green. And then I see his car—Frank's car, only I don't know his name yet. The overhead light is on and you can see him, pretty plainly, looking my way. Something draws me to it, I just start walking through what is now a mist and the slow-going car goes even slower, coming to a complete stop. He lets me inside, not saying much at first. A handsome man, sort of, strong looking. He studies a bus we are passing, one coming in to the city. Jesus, he says. It's like the whole bunch of them are looking at us.

I tell him maybe it's because he's been riding around with the inside of his car lit up. He laughs and reaches up to flick it off, and then the only thing lighting the inside is the dash. He tells me his name is Frank; he smells like Old Spice and coffee. He sees me looking at his cup, holds it out to me—You want some? he asks. No thanks, I say. I'm pretty full already. You from the South? he asks, and when I say I am, he says he can tell by the way I say I. Dead giveaway, he says, and I tell myself to address that, too, when I get the time. Maybe I could take voice lessons, or get myself a TV and just listen and practice to the local news or something, hold a book open in front of my face and talk into it, see how I sound.

We drive all the way through the city to his place, well into the suburbs. Everything is a mesh of building and roads and early morning traffic and then the buildings give way to houses and housing complexes, and the farther west we drive, the newer everything looks. I listen to everything Frank says and to how he says it. He introduces me to a woman coming out of the apartment next door as one of his nephews. Just got in from down South, he says. The lady looks pleased to meet me but is in a hurry to drive into the city, saying she hopes to see more of me later. Inside his apartment the first thing he does is phone in sick to work. I look around his place, my first Chicago apartment, see bowling trophies, a couple of employee-of-the-month plaques from some kind of drug company. Yeah, Frank says into the phone. Yeah, it came on sudden. Then he sits down on the couch and is nervous, I see, for the first time. I sit down beside him.

So what do we do next? he says. His hands are fumbling at his belt buckle, not knowing if it's supposed to be him or me who undoes it.

You don't know how it works? I say, and he shakes his head. I don't tell him I don't know either, but I think back to this one friend I had and the things we sometimes did and then I do those things with Frank. We just about all of us did these things with friends growing up, though some guys forget and others hope no one ever asks. But it's like this: when he's a certain age a guy will do it with just about anyone, especially someone close at hand. We're just guys, that's what we do, and it's not so big a stretch to do the same thing with men— they're just older bodies, that's all, more hair, a little less muscle, a little more skin, a little longer in the making. To do a man doesn't mean you've made any kind of choice in life, that your preference is etched in stone.

He buys me breakfast at McDonald's on the way back into town. Over my Egg McMuffin he tells me he wishes he could let me stay, but a lot's been going on in his life lately. My sister'll be by later, he says. She'd ask a lot of questions about you, so, you know.

Yeah, I say, I know. I think it's nice of him to offer me a place to stay and all that, if it really is an offer and not just something a first-time john says to a first-time whore. I'm pretty sure I've got Frank snowed, though, about my level of experience. But then he looks at me, says, You been doing this for very long?

I look at him, say, well, you know. And that's all I say. He smiles at me and looks pretty sad. Don't look sad, I say. Just tell yourself it's a phase.

Yours? he says. Or mine?

We laugh.

Back downtown I can see more of the buildings and streets, though fog has got the Loop, as Frank calls it, socked in. It's thicker some places than others—sometimes whole blocks will open up before you, people everywhere carrying briefcases and loaded shopping bags, men in hats and women in skirts, and you round a corner and then bam, Mr. Fog Bank. He drops me off at the Greyhound Station and makes me take three twenties. I don't watch him drive off, feeling that same tug like I felt with the waitress earlier. Inside I use the key to get my backpack out of a locker. There's every dreg in the bus station you'd ever want to see—poor people like I never saw before, bad clothes and torn-up shopping bags for suitcases. It looks completely different than at night, like in daytime every piece of dirt is visible.

I hurry back outside, telling myself I don't belong in there. And outside, as I recall, the day is sunny at last. The fog has broken. You can see all the way to the tops of the buildings. And then I see Frank's car, still sitting where he double-parked, not having driven off at all. I can see him inside it, his hand raised but not moving, like he's wondering if he should wave to me. I act like I don't see him, though—I let my eyes scan past and stay blank, not registering. I walk away, in the direction opposite Frank's car, toward the big stone lions in front of the museum on Michigan Avenue. At least this time he had the good sense to keep the light off inside his car, but that's pretty hard to tell, what with all the daylight, something I eventually learn is rare in any season in Chicago, by the lake, except summer.

Later, after the Lincoln Towncar, after a Dodge Ram too and, of all things, a Plymouth Neon, a whole lot of walking in between, I head home, tired, to get my rest—my basement room in a brownstone off Cornell, janitor's closet. Ivan lets me stay there, but not from the goodness of his heart. No, nothing so pure as that. I sleep the sleep of the dead, as they say, my dreaming moments nothing but darkness, blackness, faces of men who loom out in the night.

Then I hear a dump truck in the alley, look out my one window—only one, it's a tiny room, just big enough for a cot, a sink, couple of wash buckets, mop, period—and see that the view is getting dimmer, like it could use some Windex and elbow grease, though it may be just the sun that's going down again, maybe both. A man needs a view, I think, even if he's not quite a man yet, even if the view isn't that much of a view: It's the building across the alley I see. Old Jewish men and black men live there, alone. I see them in the windows sometimes, looking up, usually, toward the sky, wondering when the good Lord will send his angel down to take them. I turn on my one lamp by the cot, read the book of Ruth. It's the best in the whole book. The conversion part is pretty cool. Someone becomes something she was not, different beliefs and practices, but at core, the same.

I wash my face at the sink, brush my teeth, look at my lineless young face. I take my green washcloth, smell it for freshness, then wash myself, rinsing the cloth with soap again when I'm done. There's just enough light in my tiny room that you can see its colors, however colorless most of it is. From under the cot I pull the plastic trash bag I keep my clothes in, undo the twist tie, find clean clothes. I put aside three dollars in quarters, enough to do a load of laundry in the next room when I need to. When I shut the door as I'm leaving I study the Employees-Only sign on the door, wondering if it keeps people out when I'm gone, hoping that it does, but worrying more that just anyone could burst inside there when I'm asleep—someone besides Ivan, I mean.

In the big room the boilers blaze away, providing the tenants with all the heat they want. The pipes carry the rattling sound up the wall right into their apartments. Water, gas, and electric meters line the walls, an old box that says Illinois Bell. Across the room the washer and dryer sit gorged with quarters. Ivan's pretty good about emptying the machines daily, but that's not the kind of thing some desperate guy with a crowbar would know. I pull the boiler room door shut and lock it, step out onto the wet steps in my tennis shoes—good enough for Chicago snow, which is always on the ground but never so deep that you can't tread it like wearing snow shoes. Ivan is good about the shoveling of this building, too, its steps and walkways. Yes, he's good about that. I climb the steps and hop out into the alley, follow tire treads down to the end of it, then hook a left, ready to begin another glorious evening.

Then I see it at the end of the next block, my first catch of the day—SUV, family man, sitting alone and watching me as I approach. He looks nervous, looks around nervously, then pulls the vehicle up into the alley, where no one can see us. I step up to his window, which rolls down automatically, ask him what flavor he's searching for. His hands are trembling on the steering wheel, I see, and he looks at me the way they all do when they bother to look, fear and perversion lining his face at the same time. What I want to say is, Go home to your wife and kids, have a nice meal with your family and maybe, at bedtime, read to yourself from the Bible. But I don't say that, I can't, it makes for bad business, really. Let me in, I say instead; and he turns to the passenger door and reaches for the handle.

UNFINISHED BUSINESS

Standing at the graveside saying the final words over my father, Reverend Bradshaw shot a look my way, just to remind me that everything wrong in my family was my fault—he'd told me as much in a private meeting we'd had a few days before, at his office, arranged by my mother. He'd sat smugly, looking like the kind of man Hawthorne had in mind for Chillingworth, the kind who'd dog you for the things you'd done, dog you 'til you broke down in front of God and everyone. Meaningful dialogue was his specialty, but if that didn't work, he'd launch into a canned sermon and fill in your name in the blank spaces; he'd toss in one or two personal details you could think about later, sharp facts for your own self-torment. On his desk was a picture of his daughter Rebecca, whom I liked. She played clarinet in the marching band, was president of the student council, was pretty nice, really, even to me. She was okay, even if her father was a bastard. He'd folded his hands and put them up to his mouth and looked at me.

"He's dying, you know."

"I know."

"Your mother's not too sure you understand that."

"Why do you say that?"

"Because you two have unfinished business."

"Which two? Me and her, or me and him?"

He shook his head. "This isn't helping," he said.

My father had died on a cold night, but three days later it was sunny, flowers just beginning to push up through the ground.

My Aunt Liza insisted, there beside me, on squeezing my hand the whole time they were lowering the casket down with ropes. "Jesus will help you," she whispered to me. I didn't bother asking what it was He would help me with, being perceived already as impertinent by everyone that knew me. Anyway, it was just this big box they were lowering, a crate, cargo; none of it seemed real. My girl Darlene was missing in action, hadn't seen her since the night of, though I might've used some of her brand of comfort. Beside my aunt was my Uncle Fred, drunk, no surprise; he seemed to totter in the breeze that swept down off the rise of the cemetery.

"Where's the bugler?" he asked, confusing this funeral, apparently, with the last one we'd all been to, my grandfather, some kind of war hero, they told me, who'd shot down two airplanes over France. They'd blown taps for his funeral, even though he died fifty years after the war he'd fought in. Long before his funeral I remember sitting on his lap and asking if that's all he'd killed, two Germans, him pushing me off into the floor, cursing me. I didn't understand, since every week on TV the Americans killed a whole lot more than two. His son—my father—who hadn't even been to war, had often been no nicer. His favorite thing was to make me bend over, when I was small, so he could kick me just right in the ass when he was mad at me—miner's boots, steel-toed—and really, that was the least of his sins.

My brother Carl and his brood stood across the grave from me, his arm around his wife, misty-eyed as he thought about how it would be on the day she buried him, I was guessing. And my mother was standing to my left, saying nothing, weeping loudly for the benefit of everyone, just in case they'd missed the fact that she was the widow, the one filled with sorrow, the one with mascara running down her cheeks. I just stood there, taking it.

There was the singing of some hymn everyone knew, then the Lord's Prayer. Then the crowd undid itself, everyone quietly walking back to their cars. Diggers would fill the dirt in after everyone had left, as I knew from my grandfather's funeral. The last thing you saw was a big gaping hole, brown earth piled all around it. It was not pretty, but it was final.

The family cars left first. Carl drove his family in Dad's car. My mother rode with an aunt from her side. I got to ride back with my praying aunt, Liza, and Uncle Fred. Liza was Dad's sister, just a few years older than he was. Everybody stared as we left, some standing beside their cars, some inside already. We made the customary loop around the cemetery hilltop, then down the road beneath the pine trees, the evergreens, brown needles lying across the roadway.

"You'd think they'd've swept them," my uncle said.

"You'd think," my aunt said back.

His driving was steady, the careful driving of a practiced drunk. In the back seat I studied my dress shoes. I didn't bother to look at the streets and houses on the drive back; it was like I'd seen them all ten-thousand times already. Back at the house, first one inside, I phoned Darlene:

"Hey."

"Hey."

"What you been up to?"

"The usual."

"What you doing?"

"Reading a magazine."

"Come by later," I said.

"Maybe. What time?"

"Late," I said.

"Maybe," she said.

Click.

My mother was standing in the hallway behind me. She frowned. "Company'll be here in two minutes," she said. "Make sure the bathroom's okay."

"Can't they go at their own place?" I asked.

"Please don't," she said.

"Don't what?"

"Don't be such a little bastard. Not today."

She walked into the den. I just stood in the hallway by the phone. I listened to her open up her purse, dig for tissue. She blew her nose, quietly, then lit up a cigarette, inhaled deeply. Then they poured in, every old woman in town, every one with a face of grief, parched and dry and lined—partly from age, partly from bad penciling. I tried not to meet their eyes, looked instead at the phone.

"Carl!" my mother shouted out, my brother emerging from somewhere to push past me.

"You going to stand here in the hall all day?" he asked.

"Someone might call," I said.

"'Someone,'" he said. "Someone like Darlene? That trash slut."

"You ought to know," I said. "You married one."

"Just stow the shit for one day," he said. He stepped into the den, where my mother sat. I saw him put his arm around her.

I went upstairs, to my room. I looked out onto the yard at the minions pushing their way toward our house, cars all up and down the alleyway. I could see the church out the side window, my aunt and uncle's house across the street—another set, my mother's, not my dead father's people, who were generally easier to take. I fed Mack and Donna's cat sometimes when they went away, off to New York to buy clothes, coming back with tales of the City—freaks who'd tried to sell them watches or cameras or pornography on the sidewalks. The clothes they brought back were not all that nice, but they cost a lot, which was what mattered most. My brother Carl hated them—they had made him feel bad by giving him, throughout his childhood, their own son's hand-me-downs. I liked their cat, at least, a big yellow tomcat they'd rescued from the pound; they weren't all bad, obviously. I could hear the people downstairs, all the people who knew him. I could feel the floor shake beneath my shoes, milling about downstairs, then someone on the stairwell, a man, judging by his footsteps. Then his streaming piss in the toilet, just on the other side of the wall from me. A flush, the door opening.

"Samuel?"

"In here," I said—it was my uncle, the drunk one. The front of his pants were wet, but there was no point in pointing it out; he'd just make some comment about water splashing from the sink, even though I knew he hadn't used any. The piss stain made an outline against his breeches.

"Hey, what're you doing up here, little man?" he said. I was a foot taller than he was but he wasn't being ironic, just drunk, his mind stuck about ten years back when he'd towered over me and told me tales of his own youth and days of running track, going on about four-minute miles, a feat none but he could accomplish— back then, anyway. He'd given me a twenty dollar bill one drunk day; I opened up a savings account with it, dutifully, but never bothered to make another deposit. For all I knew, the manager of the bank had taken his wife out to dinner with the deposit and interest; for all I knew, he'd given it to Darlene, hoping she'd do him one cold night on his way home from the bank. She wouldn't tell me where she'd been sometimes, what she'd done—her business, really, though I wish she wouldn't've disappeared so often, rumors springing up in her absence.

"You should come downstairs," my uncle said.

I looked at him. "Why?"

"It would make your mother happy," he said.

"That's pretty low on my list," I said.

He smiled. "I understand," he said. He pulled his flask out of his hip pocket and swigged it. "Want some?" he asked. I shook my head. "This one's for you then," he said, and he took another swig. He worked hard at screwing the lid back on. "You have any breath mints?" he asked. "I have some gum," I said. He held his hand out and I pulled the last stick out of my shirt pocket.

"What'd you think of that sermon?" he asked.

"The one at the church or the one at the grave?"

"Either."

I thought. I said, "I think Bradshaw was more interested in making some people feel like shit than sending Dad off. What was all that crap about forgiveness anyway?"

My uncle laughed. He said, "He can talk, can't he?"

"He's paid to," I said. "It's his job."

He chuckled, thanked me for the gum, started chewing it; he went back downstairs, lips smacking every step of the way.

More milling feet, the murmuring of old ladies. It was awful, really, the way they sounded, a low hum to their speech brought on by the absence of hormones maybe, their not knowing any better than to gossip about their own grandchildren, figuring that you knew them, because of your age. Figuring that you cared. It was always the same shit they told, they just changed the names and dates: *"So and so's pregnant." "Is she showing yet?" "Any day now." "So and so died in the mines. Only twenty-two years of age. Left behind a wife and two young ones down to the trailer court."* Every week somebody died in the goddam coal mines. They had even set aside a column in the newspaper for the list; they called it "In Memoriam," real original. I noticed, though, they didn't bother listing the ones the mines killed more slowly, from a lifetime of sucking down coal dust. Not that I was any kind of rebel about it; I just knew that the last goddam thing I'd do on earth was go to work one mile down beneath it. That was just fucking crazy, I didn't care how much cash the mine owners from up North would stick inside your pocket, no amount was worth it.

But the alternatives blew big time. The military and then, if you survived that, continuing work for Uncle Sam down at the post office. If not that, bag boy at the supermarket like Carl and maybe, if you kissed enough ass, butcher boy in the meat department. There was college, of course, but almost no one went, since college, it seemed, led to three things and three things only—teacher, lawyer, doctor—so if you didn't want to be any of those, you were just screwed. All these futures looked real pretty. If you got to be a teacher you could be a coach, of course, but the only ones the boys and I knew tried to make you be their friends, you had to drink with them Friday nights late or just hang with them at their trailers. They'd tell you things like you need to work on your ballhandling, you need to pick up your point production—no college will take you on scholarship otherwise (not that I'd ever been scouted, received a letter, or been courted in any other way).

"Hey," a boy's voice shouted up the stairs.

"Hey, what?"

"It's me," the voice said, footsteps coming up.

"Me who, asshole?"

"Keep it down." It was Aaron, my best friend, hitting the top of the stairs. "The old lady will hear you, man."

"Like she'd give a shit," I said, gesturing to him to have a seat. It embarrassed him, that I'd say that about my own mother, even if it was true. We sat there, me and him, awkward. He looked around the bedroom at my dresser, the chest of drawers. "You have a nice bedroom," he said. "I like that Michael Jordan poster."

"Thanks," I said.

"We beat East Side."

"I know," I said. "I read about it in the papers. You got twelve points and had six assists, good game." I gave him five. The black guys we played ball with had progressed to pressing fists together, but Aaron and I were still palm slapping.

"Thanks," he said. Then he said what he'd really come up to say: "Coach's starting Donnie this Friday night."

I knew that was coming but it still hurt. "He's pretty good," I said. "He'll do okay."

"You should've called Coach, he might've held your spot."

"You know how it is," I said. "Your dad kicks off and next thing you know, you're just some kind of fuckoff."

"I'd be one," Aaron said, "if my dad kicked off."

I looked at him. "Your dad lives in Florida. What the hell do you care?"

Aaron looked hurt.

"Sorry," I said.

"It's okay," he said. "Really." We sat there in my room, him on the edge of the bed, me at my desk. He got up and didn't say anything. The stairs creaked all the way down, and then my best friend disappeared into that swell of voices. "Shit," I said to myself. "Shit, shit." I held my sides. Something was trying to well up, but I kept it down. Then my brother was in the doorway; I hadn't even heard him come up. He had a plate of food. He put it down on the desk and stood there. The plate had slices of roast beef, potato salad, a roll. There was a chunk of fruitcake on the side of it, my least favorite dessert of all time, which Carl knew, but it looked pretty, at least.

"It's artistic," I said, meaning it. I scooted the fruitcake over with my fork, cut the beef with the fork's edge. "Who made this?" I said.

"Mrs. Peabody," Carl said. I finished up the plate while Carl paced the room. He looked out my window, at our aunt's house across the street. "They're down there," he said.

"Donna and Uncle Mack?" I said.

He nodded.

"Shit," I said.

"You have to go down there sometime, you know."

"I know," I said. "This is the worst part."

Carl came over and straightened my tie, tugged at my collar.

"Do I look purdy?" I said.

"Real purdy," he said. "I'm taking mom out later. Her and that friend of hers, out to the bar. Like a wake."

"Do her good," I said.

I followed Carl down the stairs.

The testimonies came at me quickly: Every man who'd dug coal with him, every man who'd played football with him in high school, every teacher he'd ever had, every relative from every holler in Southwest Virginia, every goddam person he'd ever known, none of whom had bothered keeping up with him, every goddam one now guilty, it seemed, over having not done so, I had to listen to every goddam one and be polite and nod and grin, when the blue dog was trotted out to tell about the kind of mischief he'd done when he was my age. "Oh, my," I had to say, "that man was the prankster," or some such shit, that was the gist, anyway. I don't know what I said to any of them really. Most were so drunk they probably didn't know what I was saying back anyway, at least the men.

The women were pious enough for all of them, smug in that Sunday School way they had, Vacation Bible School written all over their pursed lips. They talked to you about how good a man he was. How he always went to church till he got too sick to do it, how he still kept up with his tithing. The preacher's daughter Rebecca and some of her friends were talking across the room and I thought about going over and saying hi to her, but then Reverend Bradshaw himself came up to me, persistent sonofabitch that he was, just in case I was starting to enjoy myself. "Your mother wants you to start coming by to see me Monday afternoons at four p.m.," he said. I just looked at him, and he held my stare. "Monday, four o'clock. Door'll be open." He walked away.

I found my uncle in a corner with a plate of food, borrowed his flask, just a swig, but then one more, to grow on. "Be careful," he said. Then I saw my other uncle, Mack, his wife Donna, walking toward me. Uncle Fred held out his plate and offered up his version of a breath mint: I shoved the piece of fruitcake in my mouth and chewed it, it tasting as old and dry as I figured.

"Son," Mack said. He looked mournful; Donna too. They were dressed in their finest synthetic fabrics, fresh off the racks from the City. I pointed to my mouth and chewed the fruitcake. Donna hugged me and got tears all over my shirt. "We're so sorry," she said. Mack shook my hand, and when I took it away, I found a fifty dollar bill in my palm. "Son," he said again. He patted my arm and the two of them left the house, having made their rounds, and walked across the street to their own pretty place. I showed Fred the bill; he laughed.

"All kinds of ways to express grief," he said, laughing.

I stuck the fifty in my pocket, thought about taking Darlene out to dinner somewhere nice, only there was nowhere nice, of course. Just a diner, a hamburger stand, a pizza parlor. You could find satisfactory, but not nice. Not in this town. Miners were not choosy customers. What mattered was the amount of slaughtered flesh on their plate. You had to have some kind of potato, too, usually mashed with a big puddle of brown gravy, though sometimes, for variety, it was gray. To feed a miner was simple; I had watched my mother do it for sixteen years.

Dinner-time always started out quiet, then came the yelling. Something was always wrong, and I was always the one who made it that way, that's what my dad claimed. Frankly, I think he was just feeling bad for the things he used to do late at night when he'd come home drunk and check in on me, things he never seemed to remember, things I never told anyone about. I was little then, but when I got big and his late-night visits ended, it was his bitching that almost killed me. At dinner one night I couldn't take it anymore. He was seriously ill by then, oxygen tank at the ready, mask dangling from it. He started ragging on me about my choice of girlfriend, calling Darlene trash and saying she'd give me the clap, and I couldn't help myself, I punched him, one good solid punch to his chin. My mother rushed over to help him up and just glared at me, but my father, he didn't say or do anything. He just sat there, short of breath, his eyes a million miles away. "Get out," my mother said. "You got it," I said.

I walked out of the house, walked the streets, seeing how other families were faring that evening. Everything was wholesome at the Weber household, the curtain on their picture window pulled wide so the entire world could see just how much they loved each other; they sat in their plush chairs and across the sofa, listening to their littlest girl play the piano. The sound of the chords came all the way out to the sidewalk—"Chopsticks"—she was good. She played it twice more, just to show how good she was, her family just as delighted each time. I moved on, not wanting to be thought a prowler. No other family looked as serene as the Webers that evening, of course, but no one, far as I could tell, was doing any kind of punching and bitching that night either. And that was the last time I talked to him. We lived under the same roof, ate the same meals, but we didn't speak. My mother filled in the silence some nights; some nights, she didn't bother. They had their own problems anyway, things they didn't need to tell me. A year passed, his lungs got worse, then he died.

Somewhere across the afternoon the funeral guests started to leave; the house was growing quieter, the murmur of old lady voices dying down. Then my mother came up to me. Her friend Sharna, a worn-out alcoholic, had her hand locked on my mother's arm. Really, she looked kind of pretty, my mother, her lipstick not too bright for a change, the mascara cleared away from beneath her eyes. "Carl's taking us out to the bar," she said. "I know," I said.

"It's just for a while," she said. She gave me a hug.

"I'll be fine," I said.

Carl said he'd see me later. I saw them drive down the alley. Then everyone was gone. Fred and Liza to the motel out at the edge of town, the miners and wives back to their houses, his old friends, all gone home, all glad still to be alive, I guess, glad this day was not in their honor. They all went home and flicked on TVs, heated up leftovers. Some young ones might've gone home and hopped in bed, if there were no kids; some older ones probably did too, to show they still could. And the old ladies went home to be by themselves, I guess. I tried not to think about them. One day my mother would be one too.

Dishes and glasses were everywhere; the dining room table was covered with food. I picked at the roast beef, ate some dressing somebody'd said was good. I sat down to read the sports page. I was halfway in before I realized that I couldn't really follow it, thinking instead about how things were when I'd been little. I told myself there had been a time when things were all right, when I actually looked forward to when he got home from work. I didn't care that his face was smeared with dust, that it looked like a mask: I thought everyone's father looked like that upon arrival, black-faced. He would pat my arm but try not to get too close, not wanting to color my clothes. He called me Chicken Hawk, Mighty Mouse, Yosemite Sam—any pint-sized cartoon character he could think of. He'd take me out to the ball court some Saturdays, help me work on my foul shot. He showed me how to center the ball above my forehead, how to line up my elbow. Things were good then between my parents. Sometimes they smiled at one another. Once or twice they even kissed.

I could hear footsteps coming up the walkway out front. I went to the door and let Darlene in.

"Hey."

"Hey."

She reached up to kiss me; I kissed her back, just a light one, a peck. I brought her in to the living room and fixed her a drink, my mother's stash.

"So," she said. "You over it already?"

She was being funny and we both knew it.

"Sure," I said.

We didn't say much. I got her another drink, got one for myself, too. We sipped our drinks.

"My mother says one day you'll get into trouble."

"That's funny," I said. "My mother says the same thing about you."

We looked at each other, laughed. Then we just sat there for a while. I switched the lamp off and scooted over beside her. I could feel her relaxing beside me, her breathing quiet but alive. It was nice, her being there. We didn't do anything. We didn't have to. When Carl brought my mother back home, the car engine idling in the alley, my mother walking around to the back of the house, I let Darlene out the front.

"See you," I said.

"I'll see you, too," she said. I gave her a kiss and then a small shove out the door. I could hear her laughing, quietly, to herself, as she walked down the steps of the house, and my mother pulling shut the back door as she stepped inside. I headed up the stairs and closed my bedroom door.

"Samuel," I could hear her shouting from downstairs. "Samuel, are you up there?"

"Yes," I shouted back.

I could hear her downstairs turning the TV on, fixing herself a drink. How could she even begin to miss him? I wondered. How would she even know he was gone? She must've been pretty drunk, the volume way up on the TV, the weatherman saying it would rain the next day and, he was sorry to say, the day after that. At three in the morning the sound of the test pattern woke me. I went downstairs and found her on the couch asleep. I put a comforter across her, turned the TV off. I tried not to make any sound as I walked back up the stairs in the dark.

MY MOTHER'S LOVERS

Sitting in the Hyde Park Coffee Shop sharing an omelette, I tell my father my mother is seeing a lesbian.

He looks at me, says, you're saying your mother is queer?

I tell him I'm not sure, I thought only men could be queer.

Not all men, he says.

No, I say, just gay men.

We had been talking about the changes in this city, like how far blacks have come in the past fifty years, the length of time he's lived on this planet. He was telling me all about Harold Washington, the mayor of Chicago many years ago—a man who lived in the very hotel this coffee shop is part of, and who ate here all the time—and then he brought up Obama, who lived just a few blocks away until he became President. We got to the gay rumors that circulated during the election, and somehow to my mind it was the perfect opportunity to let my father know about my mother's doings.

He takes another bite of omelette and looks out the window at the cars driving past on Hyde Park Boulevard. He shakes his head and says man, your mother. I can't keep up with that woman.

Then he doesn't say anything, and I try to develop my taste for the black liquid he insists on purchasing for me when we come to this shop. He won't let me dump any cream in there, no sugar—take it black, he says, the way it was meant, and he should know, he's been drinking this stuff, I would bet, since the womb—his mother's, I mean, my grandmother, who I don't even get to see anymore, not since the split. They don't talk much these days, my mother and father. I haven't seen them together in a coon's age, my father's old expression, the both of us aware of its connotations and etymology, though it's my mother, the white parent, who raises hell when she hears it.

It was a man my mother left him for two years ago, or more accurately, a man at work, her work as a university researcher which made her put in long hours and drove Dad nuts because she was never home and then he'd go out looking for her, and then he found her, one night, he told me, humping—his word—the department chair on her desk at work. Some work, he said, coming home that night and waking me up and knocking over or tearing down everything in the kitchen: plates, glasses, spices, knife holder, pots and pans and, especially, the ceiling rack. I can still see it, see him ripping down that rack. I can remember the day, years before, when my mother made him and another police officer go out and search the city for that rack and bring it home. Made them mount it up on the ceiling so she could hang all her pretty pots and pans off it and then hardly ever use them—because of work, I mean. Her work. She was busy always back then and, truth to tell, nearly always still is.

The head of city council walks into the restaurant, sits three tables away and nods to my father, one burly black man (the councilman) nodding to another lanky one (my father). Public Official Central, that's what they should call this shop, not the Hyde Park Coffee Shop, though that's a good name too. The councilman has his entourage with him, all black, that one lady with the big hat and the feather and a low-cut dress, thinking she's some kind of ebony Sophia Loren. Gray hair all of them, big guts—except for black Sophia—and suits. Nice suits, too, not the empty kind—these folks actually do stuff, make life better here for black people, at least that's what my father thinks, since it's blacks, he claims, who get the breaks these days.

You know, he says, looking over at Sophia, a black woman would never be gay.

I look at the woman too, at her heaving chest as she talks and bright red lips.

What about *Color Purple?* I ask.

That was just a movie, he says, and I tell him it was a book first, and he says he knew that, but everyone he knows thinks it's just a movie. Goddam Alice Walker, he says, saying it like she was the one who filmed it, and all by herself. And that Whoopie Goldberg, he says, spitting in that man's glass. Danny Glover should've hit her.

I think he did hit her, I say, and my father says yeah, he should've hit her, making a fist he grinds into his palm like hamburger. The councilman and Sophia share a joke and are the first to laugh, the rest of the entourage, finally, joining in—all yes-men, laughing-men. Men on TV news with opinions straight from the councilman's heart. Across from me in the meantime my father is having wicked thoughts. I know because he tells me: I'm thinking bad shit about this lesbian thing, he says.

It's all right, I say, if all you do is think it.

You're right, he says. Technically. But don't talk to me like that. You're my son, not my friend.

He's not smiling and I don't even think about chiming in. We finish off that omelette, not saying another word.

Later he calls me, asks me questions about my mother. I'm in my room trying to study and my mother and her friend are having dinner down the hall—just casual. They send me out to a movie when they want peace and quiet, what some might call privacy. That's how I know so much about Sophia Loren and Whoopie Goldberg—old movies, that's all she wants me to watch, and old stars.

I've got this small room I've had forever. I've got my bed and my desk and my computer and my bookcase, which I've had since I was six, my name etched on it in great big letters: J-E-R-R-Y. And I've got the phone up to my ear, my father's voice filling up my head, his line of inquiry completely outrageous.

Do you hear them? he asks.

Excuse me?

When they make love, do you hear them?

Do I really want to have this conversation? I ask, looking down at my trigonometry, wondering all about the triangle and angles I see on the page.

Please, just tell me, he says, and he doesn't sound so demanding then, so I tell him what I know: Yes, I hear them, every now and then. Most times, though, they send me out to a movie, so I don't have to listen.

What do they sound like?

Like two women, I say, and then there is silence on the other end of the phone. I make a few marks in my math book, the phone scrunched against my ear. I hear footsteps down the hall in the kitchen—hear plates clapping against each other, water running in the sink, catch the smell of dish detergent, just a whiff.

Is she African American?

No, I say. She's white as mom.

That's pretty white, he says. Pretty goddam white.

He pauses.

See? he says.

See what?

It's only in movies that black women do lesbian things.

There is a knock at my door, my mother, saving me from having to parse my father's logic. I tell her to come in and put my hand over the mouth-piece.

She stands in the doorway of my bedroom with her friend. Both are smiling, still dressed for work, where my mother met this "other woman," this thirtyish grad student from New York— Jewish, I think, but it's not the kind of thing you ask and you can't always tell by last names or looks.

We're going out for dessert, she says.

Where, I ask.

That coffee shop on Hyde Park, she says.

I hear my father's tiny voice buzzing up from the desk: Is that your mother? Put her on the goddam phone. Bringing home a lesbian and having lesbian sex so my son can hear!

Is that your father? she says, catching his sound, apparently, if not his words.

I give a nervous laugh. It's just a friend from school, I say— we're doing our homework over the phone.

Well, we'll be back in about an hour, Mom says. They start to leave, but then she sticks her head back in my doorway: You want to go see a movie? she asks.

I'm gripping the phone now extra tight.

Uh, maybe, I say.

There's a German film at the revival house, Mom tells me, presuming to round out my education while at the same time ensuring herself (and Susan) a little post-dessert privacy. It's set just after the war, she says. You might learn some history.

You might recall, I say, the grade of A+ on my report card for that very subject. But sure, you give me a ten and I'll hit the movie house and become even more edified than I obviously already am.

Her friend laughs and my mother reaches into her purse and digs a bill out and tells me I should watch my tone.

Why, what do you mean? I say, feigning innocence, and again her friend laughs and I shoot her a wink—she's okay really, this Susan Davis, though frankly I don't want (or need) any extra moms running around this place. One is plenty, even if the one does spend a lot of time at work, where she meets, apparently, the most interesting sort of people.

My mother comes over and puts the ten on my desk, kisses my forehead and tells me to make sure I'm home by eleven. And no gang activity, she says, this running joke we have, since she knows that my only friends are nerds as big as I am—four-eyes stuff, nice boy stuff, Obamas in the making. I listen as they pull shut the front door, then put the telephone back to my ear, like I was finally letting him breathe again, but on the phone there is only a dial tone. I think about calling him back but decide not to. He's the one who hung up, I tell myself, which means, in my world at least, that he's the one who has to call.

I check the web site, see that the German film begins in forty-five minutes. I run to the bathroom to find my electric razor, something I'm kind of growing into, but slowly, not nearly so fast as my Jewish friends, who all shave already, sprouting chest hair and other signs of manhood that betray themselves in gym class. I'm a little darker than they are but could pass for Jewish, maybe, with the right pair of glasses. They're hating me more and more these days, what with college applications growing near, my test scores and grades as good as theirs but them knowing I might have the edge on getting admitted to a top school because of my father, his blood and so my blood, at least half of it, though he was pretty light to begin with, I lighter still.

My mother is one of those Swedes from Wisconsin. She came down to Chicago for graduate school twenty years ago—Economics, earning her PhD—and thought it would be interesting to be married to a black man, at least for a while, even a light-skinned one who works as a cop and wants to fit in, as much as possible, to a broader society. I guess the culture clash finally got her though: it was a white man he found her with that time on her desk—that's about all they have working at the university anyway, only a handful of notable exceptions, Harvard always trying to lure them away. She had to find him a good lawyer that time, what with the assault charges and all. He almost killed the man, beating him with her name plate, saying my woman, mine, you devil!, over and over, at least according to Mom. Dad denied everything in the courtroom and still does. The judge was sympathetic.

As I am about to leave for the movie, I hear my father's knock at the front door. I think about not opening it, to pretend like I'm not home. And I know better than to step up to the peephole and look out, knowing he'd be watching for the light to disappear from the hole, meaning someone was inside. Let me in, he says, feeling my presence.

I open the door on the stern black man who is my father. They're not here, I say.

I know, he says. I saw them at the coffee shop as I passed it.

You saw Susan? I ask.

That the bitch's name? he says. What's her last name? Silverstein? Blumberg?

Davis, I say. It's Davis.

Well I see she's trying to pass too, he says.

For what? I say.

What do you think? he says.

Straight? I ask.

You're a smart ass, my father says. He's standing inside the apartment now and I have to ask myself why I told him about Susan in the first place. I must like trouble or something. He looks around the place, searching for signs of lesbianism, I suppose.

It looks the same, he says.

What did you expect? I ask.

Dangling beads on the doorways, he says, serious. Pictures of naked women with afros and spears.

I could see maybe a painting of Artemis or something, I say, but not any kind of afro.

Afro's coming back, he says. You'll see it when you go to school back East.

Maybe I'll go out West, I say.

No California school going to let you in these days, he says. Uh uh, not going to happen. Stay away from Texas, too, he says. Sunbelt's going to hell for black men.

What about black women? I ask.

Ditto, he says. He is pacing up and down the room. He's

keeping his hands in his pockets, making fists inside them, his blazer's tails crumpled up along his wrists. He walks beside the couch, examining the cushions. He turns quickly to stare at the coffee table, then takes a quick look at his old chair, to see if maybe his indentation has been worn away, replaced by something softer, I guess, more curvaceous.

It's the same, I say.

All the same, he says, standing in his old living room. He inhales then, and deeply. Then he exhales. He inhales again and then his eyes narrow. It's the smell that gives it away, he says, exhaling.

What smell? I ask.

New perfume, he says. Your mother only used one kind. Still does.

How do you know, I ask.

Because I slept with her last month, he says. She was still wearing it then. I bought enough of that shit to last her a lifetime anyway, he says.

And this I did not know, that my parents had been together recently. It must've been at his place.

How long's she been with this Susan, he asks.

Uh, just a week or two, I lie.

Try again, he says.

You'll have to ask her, I say, turning away, cursing my mother in my mind for being so goddam wanton. And stupid—she had to know that was the kind of thing that would have him thinking reconciliation, even if it was the unmarried kind. Across the room I see my father pick up a metal vase in his hand and grip it tight. She came by my place, he says, one night last month. She said she left you at the library. She wanted to talk, he says, about you.

Me?

He nods. She thinks we should spend more time together, you and me. That you should come over sometimes on weekends, spend the night, maybe.

I picture my father's tiny apartment. Where would I sleep? I ask.

I'm buying a fold-out, he says. Maybe one of those futon sofa things, he says. I can afford that.

And then I ask him, because I can't help but wonder: So why'd you two make love?

He puts the vase down. It just seemed right, he says. We were talking about you and we felt close for once and it just seemed okay, that's all.

I nod. He nods back.

You want to see a movie? I ask.

He looks at me. What kind of movie?

Foreign, I say.

Is it dubbed?

No, I say. Subtitled.

What color titling?

Yellow, the web site says.

I like yellow, he says. You can't read the white sometimes.

Is that a metaphor? I ask, and he has to think about it before it registers, then he smiles. You got your brains from me, he says. Your mother's got the education, but it's me that has the brains, he says, and he laughs a little and slaps me on the arm.

At my father's request we take the long way to the theater, which means we walk down Hyde Park Boulevard and pass the coffee shop just as Susan and my mother are exiting. Now it's a pretty picture and one that my father has engineered—he had to know this was a possibility, this bumping-into thing. The four of us stand there on the street gaping like fish at first and Susan, new to the fold, figures out that the black man beside me is my father.

You must be Jerome, Susan says, reaching out her hand to shake my father's, which extends forth like a piston, open and ready. I look into my mother's blue eyes in wonderment, something we almost never do, her and me, make eye contact I mean. She can tell my father's heard about Susan already—she communicates this with a look, knowing, of course, how my father must've found out. I cannot understand why she does what she does, why she is so free with her body, a way I could never be. I don't think that skin color has anything to do with it, not in a physical sense, I mean, but what do I know? I'm sixteen years old and have as yet to be with a girl, in the physical sense. Maybe it's me who's supposed to do the getting, that's what my friends tell me, the ones going away to college. They talk about finding girls who look like Susan Davis, or like my mother, the Mediterranean and the Swede, the two types, it seems, guys like most to brag about: She was swarthy and fast, they say, or, she was blond-haired and blue-eyed and my heart muscle made like an IED inside my chest. It's weird, really, having the two models for these things right there in front of you: Just picture them ten, twenty years younger and think they're not your mother, not her lover, talking to the estranged husband out here on this sidewalk in the city, in what was once a suburb but got swallowed up because the city had to grow, had to expand South and West and North, had to take on colors and hues and accents, orientations, everything and everyone coalescing into a brand-new century.

And my father does beautifully out there on the street, so exposed and vulnerable. He is open, and gracious, and once he works something through, he's about as good a man as a man can be, regardless of color, of hue, of saturation. It's all about controlling one's impulse, I suppose, of taking a deep breath before diving in to the pool, of doing your best stroke and surfacing and swimming your lane, the camera underwater beneath you, to watch you as you undulate, glide, dolphin-like. We talk for five minutes and are all fast friends, and then we have to go, my father and I, to make it to the movie on time. There is a freedom in the way he walks then, freer than half an hour ago. Now he's loose.

I like her, he says. She's nice.

She is, I say. He buys us the tickets.

You think I was going to hit her? he asks as we step inside the darkened theater.

The foreshadowing was there, I say, but I didn't really think you'd do it—it wasn't an issue, really.

Truth? he asks.

Truth, I say.

The room is completely dark and we can't see anyone sitting anywhere. We stand in the back for a few seconds like that, letting our eyes adjust, looking for a place to sit. And then the film begins, filling the auditorium with radiance. No one in fact is sitting anywhere, we have the whole place to ourselves. We sit dead center of the theater, putting our feet on the seats in front of us, watching the life of Maria Braun unfold in revival, the blond beauty on the screen looking not so different, really, from my mother.

She's a pretty woman, my father says above the soundtrack.

She's lovely, I say, and the nice thing is I can tell, as we are sitting there in this darkened theater watching this woman who looks like my mother, his ex-wife, that we do, both of us, mean it. Postwar Europe, twenty-first century Chicago—the changes come at us, big as life.

AWAY FROM HOME

At night someone can twist open a door, slip into your room, and slide a knife into your throat in such a way that you can't draw a final breath. My brother Zach taught me about the knife, something the military had taught him. He taught me about the pistol, too, and how to swim through water in such a way that no one can hear—slowly, as if you were standing, scooping your hands outward from your chest. He taught me all this down by the train trestle, at the confluence of the Cherry River. But I get ahead of myself. This is a love story, first and foremost, about me and Fred, a man I met when I was just a girl, and whom I married and who gave me a child.

We lived in Morgantown at the time, on a side street off a winding road that wound around and around a hill, like a game I had owned when I was young, where at the top, you dropped a steel marble and let it roll down and around a widening path. Tiny figures trying to make their way up the hill would be bowled over by the marble: an elderly figure with a cane was worth the least points, a mother and stroller worth more, and a child playing by itself in the road with a ball and jacks worth the most points of all. Mostly college students lived on this hill in Morgantown, our street lined with two and three-story houses that had been converted to apartments.

We had a basement place with four small rooms. It looked out onto a stone schoolyard where children played at recess like jeering lunatics, rock-throwing their main preoccupation. The kitchen had a window that opened right off a busy stairwell, and in the morning, all morning long, students with long hair and backpacks would clomp their way down all these wooden stairs toward campus, to study history, or math, or biology, or art. I wanted to be one of them but we could not afford it, Fred said, not with a young one on the way. One warm October night a man stuck his head in the kitchen window and called out someone's name, "Maxwell." I was at the stove and walked over to the window, and the man said who are you? "Janie," I said. The man looking for Maxwell looked at me closely and said that I was pretty—and it's true, I was—but I told him I was pregnant just the same, and I'd appreciate if he didn't stick his head inside our window the next time he walked past, even if his good friend Maxwell had once occupied this space.

I had met Fred at the city park in the town I call home, Shandlyville. He was part of a work crew lightly supervised—he'd done something bad once, and was in a kind of trouble. His hair was crewcut and his ears stuck out and I immediately fell for his looks, a kind of Bosco look, that monkey with the chocolate drink in old commercials. I had only to hike up the tracks behind my house for fifteen minutes till I would find Fred polishing swing-sets or laying down lime for the baseball field. I liked to watch him dig ditches best. He also mowed grass and was so good he could trim right up to the edge of the train tracks, never dropping the blade onto the jutting ties.

We walked down the hillside to the Cherry River sometimes in the evening that summer. Fred had one hour to do as he pleased, before curfew, and we found a place to hide in the shrubs. He hollowed out a nest for us, clippings everywhere, making a kind of bed. It was a time just for us, Fred said, the rumble of the train wheels rolling out to us as we lay upon the ground, the cars ferrying the black rocks to barges along the Ohio. There were ducks sometimes, in the marsh at the edge of the stream. The train whistle would blow and the ducks would lift away, their orange feet dangling. I loved Fred more than all this—more than the marsh or the train or the town itself—he could make things and make you do things you never thought you would, causing you to forget for a time what it was in this world that truly mattered.

One night just at dusk I finally told him, saying, "I love you, Fred," and he said "love," like he was mulling it, trying to shape it into something you could see.

My mother didn't like any of it. I'd come home at dusk and she'd pick the clippings from my shirt and ask me what did they mean. "They don't mean anything," I'd say.

"If your father were alive," she'd say. But he wasn't, he'd been dead five long years. My brother Zach filled in, some. He brought home a paycheck, at least, and would roam the carpet of our downstairs, restless. If I were to step into a room unannounced, Zach would spin and raise his open hands into a pair of claws. He was troubled, of course. Many of the young men of the town were, having served overseas in a place so far from their roots. But the longer I knew Fred, the more I saw of his work and listened to his yearnings, the more time I spent down by the river, away from home. He had a small book of private thoughts that he would read to me from, there inside our nest. The words seemed beautiful to me, though I'd be hard pressed to explain their exact meaning, or even to summarize what it was he had written. He called himself an artist, and I wanted to believe that he was.

He finished out his sentence, caught word of employment up north. A dream job, he said, apprentice in a glass factory, working with a blow pipe and metal stand, to roll out and help shape the gather from the fire. He would send for me, he said, when he found a place to live; he'd been gone one week when the telegram came. My mother was at the store, Zach somewhere out in the hills. I was on the Greyhound that afternoon, pregnant by the end of that month. The clinic said there was no mistaking the facts, there on the page in black and white. The morning I told Fred about our child, though, was the morning that he turned.

"I thought you were being careful," he said.

"I was," I said. "It just happened."

He looked at me hard. "Works that way sometimes, I guess." He didn't kiss me, just grabbed his lunch pail and left. I watched him walk off and then, in a panic, almost chased after him down the street. But I caught myself. I set about my chores instead.

At night in Morgantown I dreamed about my river. I would be suspended beneath the surface, my lips closed and cheeks puffed, my hair floating. My hands would be scrabbling upon the river bed, searching, reaching, and then I would wake, suddenly, agasp. You had another dream, Fred would say, his shoulder blades taut, his jawline hard. He needed his sleep, I knew, so he could be fresh for work. All I could do was say I'm sorry, I'm sorry, but the river, the river had called me and I was there.

That river. My brother Zach was such a part of it, teaching me things—things you need to know in this world to get by. He would place a knife in his teeth and swim slowly and get me to do the same, not breaking the water at all, not making the smallest sound. I got competent with the knife, learning how to catch and gut a fish precisely. I got good with a gun, but not as good as Zach, who could shoot a flattened penny from a train rail a hundred feet away.

Many evenings Fred came home coughing up the dust and fumes of his factory, the mask straps still visible across his cheeks. We made love only a few times in that apartment, always in the pitch of night, blind, but even that was ended when he learned that I was pregnant. He turned his interest to his glass, pieces he brought home from the factory sometimes in the evening, to set along the mantle of our living room. The glass things, misshapen, were always gone in the morning, as if the daylight had dissolved them. This went on for months, through the fall and all through the harsh winter they had in that town, the streets slush-piled and the students' faces hidden behind ski masks and bodies beneath dark down coats. It was a dismal time to cater to a life inside, but I thought bright thoughts as best I could, thoughts about my river and my home, the lulling rumble of its rails.

Fred had loved it, too, I know. Back in summer I had caught him by the shore gazing into the stream. He would pull cattails and prod the water, searching for crayfish, perhaps, or something buried deep in the mud. "What is it you did?" I asked, and he told me I didn't want to know. He kept a lot to himself, like where he went sometimes in Morgantown at night. I would search his clothes once he'd fallen asleep, but all I got for my trouble was an acrid smell that came from his coat.

It was almost spring, and I pulled on a sweater and walked off in Fred's direction one night as he left our apartment after dinner. When I got to the street, he was gone. I walked down a main drag and car horns honked and men shouted things till I found a side street made of brick. A prostitute walked past me and smiled but said nothing and finally I came out on the town square with bright hotels lining it. Men dressed like women stood idly beside hotel doorways, nondescript for all but the knowing few. On the square itself, homeless men Zach might have known overseas stood around metal drums with fire inside them. I saw a man who looked like Fred disappear into an alleyway. I hurried in that direction, past the false women, who murmured things, and the freezing veterans, who asked my name.

The alleyway took me, finally, down to the river, immense and churning. A tugboat squalled. I saw the glass factory in the distance, dark except for spotlights along its base. Its pipes emptied a gurgling stream of waste into the river. There was the smell of rot, and a dark figure moving along the base of the factory, tracing the stone surface with its hands. It slid around the building's edge and was gone from view. A wind rose up, carrying the river's smell.

I dreamed all night my dream about the Cherry, and woke in the morning to damp clothes; Fred was on the couch. He got his own breakfast that morning for the first time. He crunched on cornflakes and looked at me; he didn't speak, not that day, and not for weeks.

On our last evening together, he stood with the back door open, ready to speak at last. He had long since given up reading to me from his book of scribblings. I could no longer find it around the apartment, and never knew if he had given it away. Perhaps it was the trash can it found, so Fred could devote himself solely to his trade in glass. He held the doorknob and pointed. "Just leave it unlocked," he said. "I lost my key. Just leave it undone when you go to bed."

There was something in how he said it.

"All right, I'll leave it unlocked," I said, knowing that I wouldn't chance it, but letting him believe that I would.

I watched him walk down the stairs to the street, skirting by the concrete schoolyard. The sun had set but there was still some light outside. He looked so handsome in his jeans and fresh shirt, which I knew would come home stinking of the town. I ate a little something, stared a little at myself in the blank TV, read a little from the newspaper, heard the woman across the way sing her songs. Then I got ready for bed and I lay in the dark and waited.

At 1:30 I heard someone walking up our back steps. Hard shoes, different soles than the ones Fred had left in. A different step, not at all like Fred's, coming down slowly on the heel and letting the weight distribute across the toe to the tip, precise. The footsteps came up to the door and I could see a man's shadow on the curtains.

The man undid the screen door, slowly, and then twisted our doorknob, which I had indeed locked. The knob turned both ways, and then he pushed once, hard, but the door didn't give. Then he let go and closed the screen door quietly and walked back across the porch, making those strange shoe sounds. He walked beneath the porch, the stones crunching beneath his hard soles. I went to the window, in the dark, and watched him walk down the hill, the same way Fred had gone. I saw him move through a cone of a light and disappear down the street.

I hurried down the stairs. I hid by the edge of a building at the end of the street, and I saw Fred talking to the man, who pointed back to our apartment and shook his head. He handed Fred a wad of cash and walked away. Fred watched him go, then crossed the street, walking in the direction of the alley that led downtown.

He came home hours later and tried the door. I let him in.

"Who was that?" I said as he took off his stinking shirt and jeans, his shoes and socks.

"Who was who?"

"That man who came to the back door."

He looked at me. "That was me," he said.

He looked so sincere I almost believed him.

"Why did you lock the door?" he asked.

"I just forgot," I said, and he said a woman should listen to the things her man tells her, for her own good. He took some blankets and slept on the couch. I was six months' pregnant by this point, and just about to show.

I packed a bag in the bedroom. I found the hundred dollar bill I had secreted away at my mother's insistence. I waited till daybreak, and then I walked out into the living room to look at him one last time, and he looked exactly like what he was. Along our mantle sat strange glass creatures Fred had blown into creation: a fish with an extra fin on its side; an elephant with a snake for a trunk; a giraffe with squat legs, its tiny tongue darting to its chin. He called himself an artist and wanted nothing more than to create glass animals by day and wander the streets by night. I apparently did not fit that cosmology, however pregnant and askew.

I heard singing coming from the woman's house next door. It was six in the morning, and she was at her sink. The newspaper boy moved up the steps beneath her window, and made his way up to the street. I heard one thump and then another, news landing on the porches of the town.

Fred slept through it, his mouth wide, dreaming of his animals, I suppose.

I didn't leave a note. I just left, and walked down to the Greyhound station. My mother was glad to see me, and when I told her about the man Fred had sent, she dispatched my brother up to Morgantown, to see to it. I didn't think anything of it when he disappeared—he being Fred. Zach said he got Fred drunk and rowed him out onto the lake and then just left him there.

"Left him?"

My brother nodded. It was best not to press him on such matters.

The next day Zach and I went down to the trestle with a roll of pennies. He helped me make my way along the ties, as I was close with child, a child that would be his nephew. I could feel the train clicking along down the way in the rails as we laid down the pennies on the tracks, and my brother helped me off to the side as he clambered back out along the trestle. He waited till the train was just a few yards away before flying off into space. The conductor shouted something out the window and Zach looked my way before he focused on the water below, making only a tiny splash into the Cherry. The train was a long one, miles long, it seemed, pulling several hundred cars heaped with coal. By the time it was gone Zach had brought me down to the edge of the water, saying we'd pick up the pennies off the railroad ties on our way back home. "There'll be another one directly," he said, and I asked how did he know. "I just do," he said, and right then I could hear it, faint, but coming near. "See there?" he said, and then it burst into view above us, shiny and new. He helped me out into the water slowly, and then I moved the way he'd taught me to move. The child inside me liked it, I could tell. He liked everything about this place: the confluence, the black rocks, the trestle, and the feeling his mother had looking up at the underside of a rolling train.

Fred's mother, god bless her, gave me a box of Fred's things one day from the apartment. It was the hideous glass animals. I thanked her profusely and promised to show her her grandbaby. She seemed touched. My mother and I sat on the back porch that evening and watched my brother line up the animals on the stone wall and shoot them. They were so thin, they blew right apart with hardly a sound.

GROVE

B en Wallace soars with his ragged afro. He swats the ball so hard that fans at courtside have to shield their face as the ball zips past. There's only me and Vance and Joan the bartender and a couple mill workers at a table across the room. Wallace is playing the Knicks and we sit drinking drafts and eating goldfish from a plastic bowl Joan has set out, each man feeling a hum inside, something sympathetic with Wallace's moves. We watch, I think, to forget ourselves—lose ourselves, maybe, in something we could never be, afraid to try.

The phone rings so Joan answers it, says a lot of yeahs and uh-huhs, then says it's for you, Frank, and I say shit, because Wallace has just brought the Bulls back from death, as usual, less than two minutes left in the game. I hold out my palm and frown, Joan pulling the cord, walking toward me.

Swell timing, says Vance, who is thirty-five, like me, and who likes basketball too. We have been friends here in Downer's Grove, Illinois, since boyhood.

Joan slaps the phone against my flesh. Yeah? I say.

I bring you the Word, says someone trying to sound like a priest, which annoys sacrilegious hell out of me.

Who is this? I say, and when I say it I'm sorry, since I know who it is, and my nephew Paul giggles into the phone it's me, and I think this is the eighteen-year-old I only four months earlier took to the nut house in Chicago, the one whose shit I wanted nothing more to do with.

Where the hell are you? I say, and Paul tells me at a party across town, with a bunch of his old high school classmates. He's such a dumbass he don't even know those old friends of his would like to pound his face, so my night turns to crud as Paul talks into the phone, quick-dry cement across my evening. Some shave cream commercial plays across the screen now, some guy gets his face all lathered up, and Paul jabbers trash about the party and all the great young babes—he knows my weakness—and I try to figure out how the fuck he ended up there in the first place but can't. As I see it, he was locked up in the hospital and now he's unlocked, and the guys at the party will let him get drunk and high, then kick shit out of him, or worse.

My buddy Vance makes a face to me like who is it, and I shake my head tiredly, so he goes back to watch the TV, where the shave cream guy, commercial just about over, is smiling while he gets his face stroked by some blonde. Paul keeps talking away, just so much noise till he tells me Donna, my ex, is at the party, and then my stomach tightens. The phone makes static as he tosses it across the room. I hear tinny music first, then a thump, a scrape, the phone against the shag, no doubt, then I hear her voice for the first time in a long good one: You should come over, Frank, Donna breathes, her hands, you can tell, cupping the phone. She sounds truly afraid something bad might happen to Paul. She tells me things'll definitely get ugly.

How'd you end up there? I ask, and she says it's one of her and Paul's old classmates having the party, and she doesn't know how Paul found out or how he got there. I hear a lot of yelling now in the background, and I hear some guy pronouncing, loudly, the name of my nephew. Donna gives me the address; I know the street and can find it.

Vance tells me I missed Wallace make a monster jam at the buzzer that won the game, and I say so what else is new. I hold the phone out for Joan, lay a twenty on the bar and tell Vance I got to leave.

He arches his eyebrow at me: Some fun coming your way? he asks.

One never knows, I say, heading for the door. He yells I should come by his place two nights later, Wallace plays the Bucks then, and I start to shout you bet but the door is already closing behind me, and the bar, for now, is only something that was.

The cold air is waiting for me outside, and the wind. My hands instantly inside my pockets, my shoes sounding off against the sidewalk, I think about my nephew. Last summer, for who knows what reason other than I think he went crazy from smoking dope, Paul started writing what he called This is just to say notes to the good citizens of Downer's Grove—high school rich kids and their parents and a few others. It was mostly made-up stuff he wrote, but it got everyone to wondering about everyone else. He wrote shit to people like This is just to say your son gave AIDS to kids out on the playground, or like This is just to say your sister did it to the football team and they didn't even have to get her drunk. He wrote to Vance that Vance and me were fairies together, that's why we never been married and why we chum around so much. Vance and some others swore out complaints on Paul for harassment, and my sister knew we had to lock him away in the head shack, to keep him out of Joliet, or the morgue.

I hop in my car and hope none of the shit ahead will make me late for my job the next day, where I work eight to five as a lab grunt wearing a white coat, goggles and mask humped over a table, dropping solutions into people's urine. It pays the bills, and when I say that to people some ass-clown usually makes a joke like yeah, especially the water. Inside the car the ceiling light shows every line around my eyes and mouth and I hope this party is good and dark, then slam the car door against the cold. I point the Grand Prix south, remember the sound of that kid's voice as he shouted Paul's name, run only one red light and get there in under five.

The address is a trailer park, this part of town specially zoned for these big tin rectangles. One yard has a lot of Camaros and Trans Ams parked on it, so I leave my car for the concrete blocks at the door of the pink trailer. Red and blue balloons are strung along the frame and the door is covered by a sign that says ENTER PARTY HERE. This girl with blond hair opens the door and looks at me.

Are you the police? she says.

I brush past her and the party is lit up like lights at a football game and in the living room of the trailer is a bunch of kids. A stereo is on and they are all looking toward the kitchen, which you can see right into over that little wall that splits the kitchen and living room. The place is two-hundred degrees and cozy and I see four goons have got Paul pressed against the refrigerator. They're wearing high school jackets and I can tell by the tiny figures on their varsity letters that two play football and two wrestle. There's this one other short kid who's wearing a jacket that says Marching Band on it and he's got blond hair and a stud in his tongue. He is standing in front of Paul giving him shit, asking why he said all those things about everyone. I understand about half what he says, that stud a definite impediment. Nobody at the party is much older than high school, and I feel like the one adult on a field trip to the zoo. The girl who let me in is standing beside me. If you are the police, she says, could you run off that crummy Paul? She points to my nephew.

I tell her sure thing, go into the kitchen and Paul grins at me and the kitchen light shines off his braces, and I wonder how he gets them tightened at the hospital and then I remember, flatly, he's not there now—he's right here, with me, and the little sonofabitch needs me, so I act.

Look, guys, I say—the athletes and blond kid turn to me—it's all right. Paul's my nephew and he's with me.

Donna appears from somewhere in the living room and says it's true, that Paul's in my care, that I knew he was stopping by the party. I add that Paul came by the party to apologize to some people and Paul giggles there against the refrigerator. I say he's going back the next day, that he wanted to make some apologies and they let him out of the hospital to do it because it would be good therapy. Donna nods, the athletes study me.

It is easy to bullshit high school kids. The boys break up and filter back into the party, leaving only me and Paul and Donna in the kitchen. We have a seat at the dining table, which is trailer furniture, and Donna gets us each a beer from the refrigerator. She is beautiful still, and is dressed in a tight black dress that comes to just above her knees but doesn't look slutty at all. Her black hair has been permed and hangs down to about her tits and is wavy, but not curly.

You got here fast, she says.

You know me, I say. They call me Fast Frankie.

They never called me that and Donna knows it but grins anyway. I dated her when she was in high school, but now she's in college and must've just got in for spring break. The last time I heard from her was in January, when she sent me a book called *Consummation of Reality* by some Jewish guy somewhere. She said the book would explain everything about why we shouldn't see each other anymore, and in her long letter, between the lines, you could tell she'd been seeing someone at school, a guy her own age, no doubt. But I still don't know what she meant about the book explaining things, because I could only read the first couple pages without falling asleep. I tried it three straight nights, the same words, the same guy screaming at me about some kid who lives inside me, who drives me to do things but is constantly being stifled. So I slam off the alarm clock one morning and the book falls behind the bed, its final resting place.

Paul sips at his beer.

Like that stuff, huh? I say.

He shrinks up his nose and I look at him and wonder at his long hair and stupid expression how he could have turned into this thing I see.

Did you read the book yet? Donna asks me.

Sure did, I say.

She smiles this sad little smile and I try to look like I understand it.

I turn to Paul. How did you get out? I sound parental.

He grins and his lips part just a little for me to see the silver again. Signed myself out, he says. I needed a break.

I feel Donna's knee under the table and I look at her and I see that she is concerned for my nephew. She and Paul graduated together. She knew him before all this. The band kid walks in and gets a beer from the refrigerator and shakes and opens it against Paul's ear. The band kid's hair is short-cropped and sculpted with spray and he has that stud, his mouth open so everyone can see it.

Piss off, kid, I say to him.

He looks at me angrily and hangs his head and walks into the noisy living room part of the trailer, where some of the kids are trying to dance and horse around and forget me and Paul are there.

Needed a break, huh? I say to Paul. Look, these guys here want to break your face. Don't you think you should leave?

Can't, he says. No car and no place to go. He heard about the party in a text from one of the only friends he's got left, he says. He says he took a cab all the way from the hospital in Chicago and the driver was dumb enough to take a check from some checkbook Paul stole at the hospital. He says my sister don't even know he's out, and he seems very pleased with himself, and while he's telling his tale more people arrive at the pink party trailer, and I drink my beer and Donna gets me another.

This pretty little brunette wearing a Jewel supermarket frock where she must've just got off work walks in and says the trailer is her place and she don't know how Paul found out about the party but she don't want trash like him around. I start to get mad when she calls him trash because he's got some of my blood in him, my sister's, at least, but then I think I don't know what happened to

Paul, maybe his blood is bad, maybe our blood is bad. I tell Miss Jewel that I'll get him out of there, not to worry. I tell her I'll finish my beer and take him away. Five minutes, tops, I say.

Five minutes, she says back to me plainly.

Jewel says hello to Donna and then Donna introduces me and then Jewel smiles and says she's heard all about me and Donna blushes. Donna says, I told you that two years ago, and by the way she says it, you can see in Miss Jewel's face she figures out that things must be over now. So they talk about college for a while and Jewel says she's thinking about going to a city college next fall and asks Donna how she likes Champaign-Urbana. Donna says U of I is great and that she's majoring in psychology and I remember the book she got me and imagine that the dust bunnies have had their way with it for weeks now.

In the living room some guys are taking turns trying to tape a Johnson and Johnson cotton ball to the ass-end of a Playboy centerfold. They wear blindfolds and spin themselves around maybe five times and then head off, all at once, to where they think the picture is.

Look at those morons, Paul says to me, the boys lumbering off into the crowd, looking like they might dab away someone's pimples.

It's that new, tall fleshy model everyone loves who's spread out there on the wall, with her chest pooched out and they never show her ass, you know, which tells you something, and they say she looks like Monroe but that's hard to believe. Nobody looks like Monroe, though some might try, and no one, absolutely no one can beat the way she looked in that *Asphalt Jungle*; she was younger then, softer, and the camera didn't need to pull any of that soft-focus shit to make her face look good. I watch enough late night TV to know. Finally a wrestler, tall, tabloid, connects the cotton and his friends, even the girls, hail him like he's some kind of party genius. His blindfold half off, he grins like the pirate goof he is.

I think this is pretty funny, maybe it's all the beer I drunk at Joan's place, and I chuckle and then Paul starts giggling and I look right into his face and we both are laughing about nothing. Paul's long hair shakes and I wonder if they let him listen to that metal shit he loves so much in the hospital but I am still laughing. Donna and Jewel stop their talk about college to stare at us.

I load Paul into the back seat. His medication might have mixed bad with the beer or maybe someone slipped him a pill because he started to get slurry real quick there in the kitchen of the trailer. Donna helps me and she has on her coat and snow has started to fall and things are covering over. Her daddy the doctor got her the fur coat for Christmas, three months back, and I wonder if she'll bother to keep up with all these low-class kids inside and then I wonder why she ever dated me. I guess I seem pretty slick to a sixteen-year-old, but they figure you out eventually.

Paul is passed out in the back seat and Donna rides up front. I get the wipers going full. I'm taking her home, to this fancy subdivision where her family lives. I can remember when this whole town was only a couple of houses on the prairie with a train running through and a few farm houses and then more houses moved in and more till it seemed like every white person in Chicago had left the city for the prairie. Donna sneezes a dainty little sneeze and I say God bless.

She is I think the only person I know whose family is together still and who nothing awful ever happened to. She is a happy person in general, which is what attracted me to her.

It's too bad about Paul, she says.

What?

Paul. It's too bad about him, that he lost it and you had to put him away.

Yeah, it is.

What are you going to do with him?

Take him home and let him sleep it off. Tomorrow bright and

early I'll call his mom and the two of us will take him back to Michael Reese.

Oh, she says.

I turn down the windshield wipers a notch because it's only those big flakes gliding down now, and not too heavy. Paul is snoring loud in the back seat. Did he ever write you one of those notes? I ask.

No, she says.

I guess there's not much bad he could say about you, I say.

She looks over at me and I feel her smile; I keep my eyes on the road because the streets are full of snow and people die out here sometimes. The windshield wipers squeak.

Donna asks, Did he write you one?

I tell her no, but he wrote one to Vance about me and Vance.

What did it say? she asks.

Guess, I say. Maybe read some more books and it will come to you.

She turns away and faces out to the wet streets. Two years ago she'd've said something in defense, but now she doesn't bother to insult me.

In her driveway I help her out of the car and try to kiss her. She seems stronger than I remember and she pulls back. But then she looks into my face and leans against me for a hug. I slide a hand between the folds of her new fur coat and push between her legs at the knees.

What is this? she says.

She pushes me against the car and walks through the snow in her black pumps. I never tried anything like that before. I thought maybe it would help. She does not look back and the big white door with no windows closes, the porch light goes off.

At home I load Paul onto the couch and leave him sprawled out. I wash the night's grit from my face with this anti-aging soap and then put my hand over the lightbulb above the mirror, dimming the light, seeing myself the way I want me to be. In my room all at once I get down on my knees and start fumbling beneath my bed, clearing away old socks and a t-shirt, and I look for Donna's book but can't find it. It is lost to me for now, so I get into bed and stare into the darkness, and I hear him, near daybreak, fumbling around in the bathroom.

What are you doing? I yell.

Flossing my braces, he says.

He says he's lighting out for the territories, thumbing down to Missouri maybe, or Arkansas. I tell him I have a gun and that if he tries to leave the house I will shoot his goddam thumb right off. He gets quiet in the bathroom and I pull the gun from beneath my pillow and cock it and know the sound carries down the hall to him. In an hour I call his mom and we take him back to Reese. I help sign the papers at the nurse's desk, and then out in the hallway, just after they take him off, I let her hold onto me as she is crying. She thanks me and tells me it's hard without a man around, but at least Paul's father carries her and Paul on his insurance still. Paul's father dumped my sister five years ago and moved up to Lake Forest with his secretary, so I've been kind of a father to the kid. Until all this crazy-shit happened I took him to movies sometimes, and out to the malls and all that. I could never get him interested in ball, though, which is too bad, because it might've helped with his discipline.

I get back home from the city and get ready for my job at the piss lab as quick as I can. I have to iron one of my white coats and can't find a belt anywhere, thinking maybe Paul stole them when I wasn't looking, and then as I am about to shave I find the note inside the medicine cabinet: Dear Franklin: This is just to say thanks for the swell time, you fairy. Say hi to Vancey for me. He signs it The Word. I crumple it and watch it drop to the waste basket, then I pick it out and uncrumple it and tear it apart into a million little pieces. All day long at work they ask me what's wrong, what's wrong, and I just tell the part about signing the papers and my sister crying.

The next night at Vance's we are watching the Bulls. Wallace has four blocks and ten rebounds already and the game's barely into the second quarter, and I am admiring his immense talent and I tell Vance that Wallace seems like someone you'd like to get to know, but Vance doesn't answer. He just sits there beside me on the couch, watching the game. Then I get this crazy thought and start to wonder if maybe I like Ben Wallace too much, and I tell Vance this and say maybe my nephew is right about me. I think it's half funny, at least, but Vance isn't laughing. He stares at the TV instead, and then he asks, without looking at me, would I like a back rub to help quiet down. I try to laugh some more but Vance isn't laughing. He's just sitting there beside me. His mouth is half full of popcorn, I know, but he stops chewing.

Look, I say, I'll see you later. I just remembered I have to be at work early tomorrow. As I grab my coat and head for the door Vance shouts at me to think about why I am thirty-five and not even close to being married. Yeah, well, I start to say, and then I just shoot him the bird and leave.

I drive into the city. It is midnight and then two and then four o'clock and I ride up and down Lake Shore Drive a half dozen times. The road is wet here where it only is raining because the lake keeps the city warm for a few miles in. I see the Wrigley Building all lit up on the river every time I pass by the place where they straightened out the big S-curve on Lake Shore. Lights flash red on top of the Hancock, warning planes away. I get a cup of coffee and gas twice at an all-night station in Roger's Park. When the sun starts to break on Lake Michigan and I can see the gulls flying low across the dark water, I cut across Jackson through Grant Park by the dead fountain, over the train yards, across Michigan Avenue and on west to State. State Street is marked off these days for only buses and taxis where they got an outdoor mall. Every now and then some clown will drive a car down it though, not like when I was a kid and we used to come into the city and I would stare at the black people while my parents dragged me from Carson Pirie to Marshall Field's, cars all over the place.

I drive up State Street, which looks deserted at daybreak, and get to the stoplight at Madison. When I was a kid Dad told me this corner was the zero point of the city, the place where the city divides itself, north and south, east and west. I look at the stores north of Madison, then south, then east and west. Every window has some kind of flashing display, which stands out against the wet sidewalks and grey buildings. I sit right there in that spot and wonder why I only date girls younger than eighteen, and why they get younger every year. At least the girls don't expect much. It is hell, though, trying to get the parents of a fifteen- or sixteen-year-old to like you.

A blond-haired kid in a leather jacket comes up to my car from somewhere off the street and I think at first it is the band kid from the party two nights back, but this kid is younger. I roll the passenger window down and he sticks his blank face into my car. He looks cold and wet from what is now only a drizzle.

What do you want? I say to him.

His eyes flash a little, some personality taking shape. He grins, and then says to me, That's supposed to be my line.

Get in, I say to him.

Deep down it's like I've been here before, sometime, somewhere. We ride down the street as the buses bring downtown the first load of workers, bringing them in from the South and West of the city. From inside their bright-lit domain they look down at me, their dark eyes watching.

ONE DARK SKY

My father looked like anyone else. A little taller maybe, stronger, more handsome. Neat but not too neat, pretty close to normal. To most people, he was just a teacher—math, science, physics—which he was, at a Catholic school on the South Side. With a piece of chalk, standing in a suit and tie in front of a blackboard, pointing to some equation, he seemed like a typical educator. But at night, come dark, that's when he changed, and went about his real work. His targets were always the same. Middle-aged, pretty good shape, just regular guys, except that most of them seemed to live alone. He'd leave me in the car and go up to their apartment and then, half an hour or so later, he'd come back with certain signs: face flushed, hair damp, eyes flashing in all directions, like there'd been some kind of struggle.

You never know about some people till it's too late. Like at the end of *Invasion of the Body Snatchers*, the original, when Kevin McCarthy is lying in a puddle in that cave with Dana Wynter, hiding beneath the floor boards, staring up through the cracks at all the running legs and flashing crotches and yelling voices. When the snatched people of Santa Mira finally leave the two of them alone, he tries to prod her into running for the highway. She's so tired, she says, can't they just sleep for a little while? But he knows they shouldn't sleep, he tries to kiss her awake, and the camera gets right in his face as he pulls back and looks at her, wide-eyed, because he knows, and now we know, that she's become one of them. My God, he says, you fell asleep, and she tells him that yes she fell asleep, and she likes what's happened to her, the change. Or maybe it's like in vampire films, at the end, when the main guy, after killing off a dozen vampires with wooden stakes and silver bullets and sunlight, finds out that the woman he's dragged across the castle to safety turns out to be one, too. You know the scene: mayhem and bodies everywhere, the man takes the girl in his arms and says something like darling, we're safe at last. Then the camera moves around to the back of his neck, where you see the girl's sweet face has turned all forehead and fangs. Freeze frame. Sometimes you hear a scream over top of the final image—or a yell, I guess, since it's a man who's doing the screaming. It's supposed to be a surprise, of course, but sometimes it's no surprise at all. It all depends on the audience, and what they want to believe.

My father bought me comic books before we'd go by an apartment, and I had a special reading lamp that clipped on to the dashboard. If it was winter he'd leave the engine running, the heat on. Sometimes I'd get sleepy, probably the exhaust. We parked on Harper a few times, twice at Kimbark Plaza, but mostly on Scarborough Road. Waiting in the car I read about war: about men in foxholes fighting Nazis, about German hand-grenades called potato mashers, about Thompson submachine guns and pineapples, Japs, Midway, Guadalcanal, Berlin, the Rhine River, Paris: It was his hope that one day I'd come to love war so much, I'd enroll at West Point. Strange dreams for a vampire, I thought.

My mother didn't know about his other life, I guess, his night life, his wet-haired, face-flushed time of the evening, or if she did know, maybe she pretended not to, for my sake, just as I too pretended. Sometimes at night I'd get up to pee, and I'd pass by the living room and see him sitting in the chair, facing out the window, looking up at the stars. Usually, in Chicago, you couldn't see boo out those windows, but sometimes the clouds would lift and there he'd be, in the dark, staring out. He never heard me, I'm pretty sure, and I'd go ahead down the hall and shut the bathroom door quietly and pee in the dark, sitting on the seat, the way my mother had taught me. (She got tired of cleaning up our mess from the tiles, and for years she nagged until my father and I learned how to sit, just like she had to do.) When I passed back by the living room, he'd be gone. Sometimes we'd be sitting there, the three of us, in the living room after dinner, and my father would say to her, he'd say, I think I'll take Johnny out to buy a few comic books. My mother would look up from the *Tribune*. That's nice dear, she'd say, father-son bonding's always a good thing. And she'd hurry us out of the apartment, so she could spend quality time with the Life section of the newspaper.

Conversion always figures into these things. Sometimes someone is not a vampire and he has to be turned into one, before he can go about his own vampire business. Sometimes, though, the transformation takes time, like in *Lemora*, about a woman vampire who lives in a house in the country and keeps her doors locked at night because outside, men who have become half wolf roam her estate. She explains to a young girl she's taken in that the wolfmen are failures, they didn't turn out the way they were supposed to. And it's not like my father became wolfen or anything, but I began to notice a change in him when the new math teacher showed up at school. Mr. Kent had this strange look about him, he was shorter than my father, and his hair was too dark. I'd see him in the hall sometimes, outside my father's door, just waiting. I'd hear him ask my father a math-teaching question, like the best way to explain about pi, but it didn't look to me like he was really listening to the explanation—Mr. Kent seemed more interested in smiling, and making some weak joke. Sometimes he'd invite my father off-campus for lunch, my father bringing home the sandwich my mother had made for him that morning and leaving it on the counter. Then he stayed with Mr. Kent after school a few times, talking about teaching, he said, sending me home by the bus and getting home later and later.

It started to trouble my mother, and one night, after a few weeks of Mr. Kent, my mother and father talked with the doors to the living room drawn shut. I heard yelling, screaming, and then the next morning everything was quiet, no one was talking to anyone, so maybe my mother did know. She'd spent the night on the couch, which I wasn't supposed to see but I did on my way down the hall to the bathroom. Funny, what you see when no one knows you're watching. Like Mr. Kent and my father secreted away in a dark corner of the school building, talking quietly to one another, their faces inches apart, thinking no one is there. And funny what you see, too, right in front of your face: the things people let you see, thinking you won't ever understand. Mr. Kent, coming up to my father in the hall and putting his hand on my father's, my father smiling but then remembering where he was. You tell yourself it's the kind of thing the undead do, then you tell yourself again, to be sure. There were other boys at the school, whose fathers were teachers too, but not like mine. These boys went about their days, their heads in books, not needing to be watchful. I tried to move through the halls the way they did, eyes down, a regular kid, not one with a vampire at home. Mr. Kent got transferred, eventually, to another diocese, and by then my father and I were into the comic book buying phase of our relationship.

The real fear with vampires, of course, is that you could turn into one yourself. I mean, your father's one, so why not you? One night you go to bed all normal, the next morning you wake up with a sore neck. It happens in your sleep, in your dreams. The next thing you know you're like poor Kevin McCarthy, when he reaches the highway and starts screaming at the cars stuck in traffic: They're here, he yells, you're next! I mean, my father wasn't, then he was. The change just seems to happen.

One time my father told me he wanted to visit the apartment of this man he'd met that day on the train. I'm not sure about this one, he said to me as he handed me my stack of comic books.

What do you mean, I said, and he told me oh, never mind, he'd said too much already. He hurried off to the apartment upstairs, disappearing in the hallway. I sat in the dark for a while, watching the door, waiting to see if my father would come back right away. After a few minutes I turned on my reading light, and began to read about the allied invasion of Sicily. Then I heard a sound at the window, and looked up and saw a squeegee man cleaning the windshield on the driver's side. He'd surprised me, coming out of nowhere. He wiped the window clean, and the entire neighborhood came clearly into view, bright and glistening. Up in the sky I could see Cassiopeia and Cepheus, Orion. Then the man came around to my window. God bless you, he said, and he held out his hand and I rolled the window down and handed him the comic book about Italy. He held it up to the street light and laughed and then he walked away, tucking the comic book into his back pocket, and I moved on to the next one with the window down, listening to the sounds of traffic on Scarborough Road as I read. Finally my father came back to the car with a flushed face and wet hair. When he got inside the car and the ceiling light came on, I could see that there was blood on his lower lip. What happened up there? I said. Nothing, my father said. I was just talking to that man I met on the train. That's all. At the stoplight the same squeegee man as before came up to clean our window, not recognizing us, apparently, as a car he'd done just half an hour earlier. He leaned over the windshield and looked inside, saw my damp-haired father, then hurried away to the next car in line.

I saw the man from the train for the first time a few days later, in the delicatessen across the street from his apartment. At least that's who I think it was. It was daytime. My father and I were taking home roast beef sandwiches so we could watch basketball on TV, more father-son bonding, I guess. Roast beef on Kaiser rolls, hot mustard, lettuce, tomato, and onion. I saw the man walk out of his building across the street into the deli while my father and

I were standing there waiting for our order, and I saw my father see him, his face flush, his eyes change. Go to the car and wait, he said to me, and I did and then watched the two of them through the window. The train man kept crossing his arms and shaking his head while he listened to my flush-faced father, but finally nodded, like he agreed with what was being said. Then my father came out to the car.

At home, during the game, he chewed his sandwich but his mind didn't seem to be on the game or the roast beef. He was thinking of the evening, I guess, and what he would do at that time. The game was close, right down to the final buzzer, but my father didn't bother with his usual comments, like why basketball was a better game when he was my age. And then at dusk he announced to my mother it was time for more father-son bonding. My my, she said, a whole day's worth. A short while later we pulled up outside the train man's apartment. My father went inside, and I got out of the car and hid beneath a maple tree and scanned the windows till I saw them. They were talking to one another frantically up in the window, and then the train man came over to the window and pulled down the shades. You could see their shadows on them, just like in movies on Sunday afternoons.

My comic book collection grew. *Sgt. Rock, GI Joe, Nick Fury.* Zeroes blazed down from the Pacific skies and went rat-a-tat-tat; sand kicked up down below, where the American soldiers lay. Panzers rolled down hillsides going clack-clack-clack while dog-faces leapt onboard them, tossing pineapples inside and waiting for the bright explosion. The stories always turned out the same, some guy gave his life and the Americans won, the Germans or Japanese lost, everyone was happy in the end. It was hard to think about West Point when everyone who fought was just a grunt. Regular guys. G.I. Joes. But on Sunday afternoon, when I was home alone, the horror films came on, a welcome antidote. Charlton Heston with a rifle and a scope firing down on the walking dead in the street below; video game precursors, one normal man against everyone else who was, all around him, changing into something he did not want to be.

Then one day without a word the comic books just stopped. My father began to stay home again in the evenings, and he and my mother began to talk again in full sentences. He began to look like anyone else's father, even at night, when he and my mother studied the *Tribune* for things to do on the weekend—first-run movies, plays, opera. At school the other boys still walked the halls, their heads in books, their fathers waiting at the end of the school day, like mine, to take them home. I still watched the movies on TV, reruns of reruns and knockoffs of the originals. There was a remake of the Kevin McCarthy movie, and it wasn't bad in general except they ruined it when they showed exactly how the change takes place, how the seed pod extends forth vines to drain away the life force of a human. It looked pretty painful, really, and I felt like I didn't need to see it. I liked the mystery of the first movie better, not knowing exactly what takes place to bring about the change.

GRAND FORKS

Sonny Jane wasn't mean exactly but he did take a kind of glee in perpetrating certain acts. Like wrap his arm in gauze and douse it with catsup, then tumble to the kitchen floor splattering thick gobs of red. Turning from the sink that time to see, his little brother let loose a shriek that could melt linoleum.

Or Sonny would be sitting in bed, projector on a page showing the Creature, tall and green and frog-like along the wall.

"Hey, Todd. Come here."

Sonny would wait for it—the footsteps, then stopping. Knowing his brother was at the door, pushing it slightly.

"Yeah?"

And then the scream.

This time Sonny stood in his room, tight jeans, T-shirt, gloves. And the ski mask, brown wool, red stripes around the eyes. He made a boxing move toward himself in the mirror—one, two, real quick—and then pausing to assess his stance and over his shoulder seeing the slightest sliver of a face in the barely open doorway, down low. Sonny spun, lunged, laughed to himself at the sound of running feet.

In his father's green Ford truck he drove. Ancient thing, from the 40s. Everyone in town of a certain age knew that truck—Jane would take it out to the highway in late August and sell the ears. Stand there in his bibs, no shirt, handsome and tanned.

Jane's son drove along the river road, three houses in a row, Sandersons, Fettsteins, and Mahoneys. Dumb fucks every one—

too dumb to move, flooded every damn year. Nighttime and they were lined up on the porches in their chairs just rocking away and right under the train tracks, beside the posts that held them up, he saw the one.

He squalled the truck and got out.

The one looked at him. Put his hands up. Shook his head. The way the Sandersons told it, the man in the mask beat shit out of the Benson boy. Punched him in the stomach. Doubled him. Put his hands together like a club and drove down on the back of the Benson boy's head. The man kicked the boy a few times as he lay unconscious—twice in the crotch, once on the chin, young Benson's head snapping back. The Sandersons called the police, who called an ambulance, the Ford long gone by the time the med-techs arrived and stood there gaping—the fat one whistled, like man, someone done whupped this white boy really good.

Sonny sat doing math, Quadratics. They were easy, and the telephone rang.

Mr. Jane went to the phone on the hallway stand and at his desk Sonny pretended to write numbers, essentially going over the "6" again and again, the paper wearing thin as the number six thickened.

"No, I was not out in my truck. Thing's been in the garage for years. Huh uh. No sir. No way."

Jane pushed his son's door open and saw him working his math. The boy wouldn't look up.

"You can come by if you want. Check the truck yourself."

He put the phone gently in the cradle.

His son looked at him.

"You been anywhere tonight?"

"Walking," Sonny said.

"Anywhere else?"

Sonny looked away.

"All right. Come out to the pasture with me."

They walked to the end of the property, toward the structure at the edge of a big field the father had sold and to which nothing had yet been done. Word had it one day it'd be a trailer court for Natives called Grand Forks, not because they were anywhere near North Dakota, but for the view of two washes that joined at one corner of the field, the only flat land in the valley (such as it was— more a confines) that didn't flood in heavy rain, thanks to really steep banks of rock that would not wear.

They stopped by the garage, the father pointing at tire treads through the tall grass—one set leading out, a second leading in.

"You want to tell me what this is?"

"What what is?"

"The treads. Thought you went for a walk."

Sonny looked off, finally said, "Good walk from here to the house."

"Did you maybe take the truck for a spin?"

"Could be," Sonny said. "Been a long day. Hard to remember every activity."

The father put his hand on the green hood, though there was no need—you could still hear the old heat shields contracting with tiny tocking sounds.

"How'd she run?"

"Good," Sonny said.

"Benson boy's in the hospital. Concussion. Maybe some brain damage. He's not awake yet."

Sonny didn't comment.

"So you finally heard?"

Sonny didn't answer. But yes, he'd heard the rumor, finally, that his child to be was the Benson boy's. Sonny was 16, Benson only 15, the girl younger still, but of age, at least in this state. Sonny and the girl had been shotgun-wed a month back, she living out by the river road with her parents, the four adults trying to figure living arrangements, once birthage commenced.

"Get the mower out. Grass needs mowing out here."

"Tonight?"

"Got a light on it. You'll be fine."

They lived far away from any neighbors who might catch the sound of a John Deere in the night.

Mrs. Benson sat in the hospital room beside her boy's bed. There hadn't been a Mr. Benson for some time. But she did have a daughter and another boy, and the girl was back home watching the young one.

The woman did not dye her hair and had a sandy brown these days instead of the dark brunette of her youth. While not young, she still looked good; her kids took after her, and all the girls were crazy about the Benson boy.

"He'll probably be okay," the doctor said.

"You think?"

"Probably."

She nodded. She brushed the bangs off his forehead.

"You know what he wants to be?"

"Huh uh?"

"A doctor."

"Smart?"

She looked at him. What a question. She said, "How smart do you have to be?"

The field was lit up by flying bugs. The boy watched his brother riding back and forth on the Deere in the patch of high grass in front of the old garage. The boy had the mask on he'd seen his brother wear earlier. He was waiting for just the right moment. There were 10,000 stars at least.

August.

You just knew something was going to happen, and it did.

Not the little brother jumping out and scaring the brother on the Deere before losing a foot in a bloody spray.

Not the Benson woman weeping by the bed of her dying son—the Benson boy would be fine and would in fact go on to be a doctor, though he would have to study at an off-shore school for his degree.

Not the pregnant teenager hearing the news of the beating and breaking down and confessing her own sins to her mother.

Not the mother of the boy mowing on the tractor and the one hiding in the weeds, telling her husband what an awful job of fathering he'd done.

Not the doctor in the break room drinking his cup of coffee and perking up just enough to realize how badly the Benson woman had just insulted him.

Not the father of the boy on the tractor and the one in the weeds, pulling down a bottle of rye and drinking himself drunk.

But the Sandersons, excited by the beating they'd seen earlier and the police questioning after, going at it on a hot August night. Rotund, bad heart—you can guess the inevitable. And then the floating up of Sanderson looking down on his wife's pretty face— still pretty after all these long years and maintaining her shape while he had larded up. She looked at his body puzzled, Sanderson saw, and then she shook it, lightly at first. He wished he could say or do something—something to calm or comfort her—but he was floating away, right up through his attic, which was a mess and had been for years, thanks to their having moved into it all the secondary things they'd accumulated around the house, saving them from the floods—he'd stuck her with all this junk and felt a pang. He floated out past the big rocks and out by the hospital and saw in the tiny window the doctor flirting with Mrs. Benson— actually the doctor'd put his hand down low along the small of her back and was right up close to her face, and she was taking that hand and putting it back where it belonged. She turned to get something from the break room's refrigerator, back side protruding nicely (she was aware), and the doctor this time only looked. And then Sanderson floated by Jimmy Jane's farm, where he saw the older boy mowing the old pasture in the dark and the small Jane boy in the weeds pulling off the wool mask because it was just too hot on a dank August night for such a joke.

The last thing on earth that Sanderson saw was a tiny drama with the boy trekking into the house and being stopped by his mother, who took the mask and stuck her hand inside and pushed two fingers through the eye sockets, wriggling them.

He was drifting farther but he saw her carry it to the sink and take a butcher knife to it sixteen times at least and feed the pieces one by one to her disposal, which roared in the night now that the mowing was done and the heat shields on the green Ford had cooled and it was Sanderson floating up to the heavens, wondering at the things of this world and thinking more than anything that it was all of it kind of funny.

And the boy, the little one, upstairs with that projector finding a picture of a naked woman to show on the wall for when his brother would walk inside the house but it was the mother who saw first and slapped that boy ten ways to Jasper.

LEOPOLD AND LOEB

Some of that shit Paul knows surprises me. Like how he gets past the guard with a hundred dollars. Two fifties folded twice, rubber band down the second fold, strap it to the underside of his nuts. Paul knows Whitey, the Negro guard, gets squeamish doing more than run his hands up and down your rib cage and hips, bang them flamboyantly, maybe give your pocket a squeeze, more pantomime than serious search. Paul chuckles as we head through the doorway, into the March sunlight and chill wind, Whitey's voice telling us to have a nice walk, but to get our asses back in fifteen. Yeah, right, Paul says to me. Paul got the plan from one of those memories that bubble up inside his head, some plotline from a comic book. Every day a guy and his girl motorcycle up to Checkpoint Charlie, *Guten tag* the guards, Paul says, at the watch tower, cozy up so that when they make their break, jump the bigfuck wall like Steve McQueen, the guards won't shoot, at least not right away. The hidden camera whirrs as it follows us down the concrete walkway, clicks as it turns to follow our turn, left and down the street. Got the shit mounted on every doorway, Paul says. Have a room ... men who watch monitors.

Uh huh, I say.

We walk casual, not glancing back. Be cool, Paul says, but I know I can be, and don't need to hear it, really, his advice, though he is maybe saying it out loud for himself, and I am just along for the listen. Then halfway down the block our moment has come and Paul shouts Fly, motherfucker! He breaks into full run, me following, and from every doorway every camera clicks like so many metronomes for the hearing-imfucked, our feet pounding out their time. We caper down Cottage as the Number 4 rides up, jump inside as its doorway closes with a fat gasp, and the driver, driving, stares ahead as Paul pulls two tokens from beneath his tongue and drops them into the box. We walk down the quiet aisle, along the black mat between the rows of seats, find one empty and sit, the only white people on board. I listen to us breathe while Paul does something with his fingers, taps the thumb against every digit in turn, enumerating who knows what, and I mean this completely literally. Then he groans. See what they did, he says, pointing out the window. He means the shrubs at the end of the grounds. Each one has been cut like a box since last we walked, conformed to some notion of order. They cream-cheesed the sonofabitches, too, Paul says, and I believe it is the snow he is referring to, laid on top of each big cube, evergreen with white frosting, somebody's birthday platter, maybe. We can talk about them later, I say, and Paul contains himself by chewing on his knuckle.

Outside my window the ghetto begins, burned out buildings and bulldozed parking lots, some snow-covered, others littered with old piece of shit cars, windows broken, cobwebbed from rock impacts. Through here the bus makes no stops, since here almost no one lives, and we make good time, blocks peeling away. Then at the projects blue drapes flap in the wind, foregrounding tall yellow pillboxes.

They look just like the Dunes, Paul exclaims, drawling out the vowel in dunes like some skinny Ralph Cramden. Bus ladies with shopping bags and thick eyeglasses look at him, at us. One looks back toward the hospital, then back again at Paul, who squirms in the seat beside me.

Oh, yeah? I say, casual, looking out the back window for marked cars.

Paul grins, looking this morning only half maniacal. He says, My parents used to take me and my sister there, Joe, to the Dunes in Indiana. It's like a big beach for all those Hoosiers.

I see.

In summer, we'd ride there on the train.

I bet.

It was nice, he says. Best time of my life.

I don't doubt it, I say, speaking in a quiet voice, not wanting the one old lady to figure us out. She's the kind that calls the cops, the kind who'd get off the bus, special, just to slip a quarter into the pay phone, whisper you out. Both tall, she'd say, both white, one jacket orange, the other red.

At 55th Street Paul pulls the wire but the driver won't stop till 57th. The bus drops down on its side toward the curb, its back door hisses open. It is ten blocks or more, I know, to the train station, and Paul's never been in Hyde Park, he says, but I know it well enough. We hurry across the street, lose ourselves in the crowd along block two of 57th, not wanting to hang out on Cottage, the first place they'll look. As we walk we pull off our jackets, reverse them, mine changing from red to blue, Paul's from orange to black. The weather's not bad, the temperature right around freezing, the sky sunny, blue. We slow at the Gothic buildings, stone-thick and angular, students moving in every direction, crossing our path, Paul claims, in Xs, Ys, and Zs. We open ranks for a Chinese girl, dark hair, dark eyes, then close again as her perfume sidles against us.

Nice, Paul says.

We pass three-story brownstones, then beneath a building that has, on its corner, an observatory. Like at night they could see right through these street lights, I say. Hah, Paul says, and at the stop sign he points down Ellis, where I see only tennis courts, some statue beside them. Sixty years ago, he says, beneath that clay they triggered the world's first atomic reaction. Something you read?

I say, and he says yeah, then wanders off like a zombie, leaves me standing there for a full minute, walks north while I am pointed east, to go see that globby statue by the courts. He stands before it and gesticulates like he is in the presence of a greatness. Hey, I yell down the street, not wanting to use his name, just in case. Some students look at me. Hey, I yell a second time, and he makes some kind of touchdown sign as he is looking at the bronze thing, he may be blessing it, for all I know, and then he turns and walks back and gets in path with me again, grinning, remembering our plan. I forgive him this deviation, since he's such a big fan of World War II. He knows all about Los Alamos, and about Nazis, can name every city that housed a concentration camp. One whole week at the hospital for something to do he wore a pink armband, till the doctor made him take it off, saying it wasn't funny, not funny at all. But the doc didn't see the joke of it: Paul wasn't trying to be funny, he was just being Paul, just as surely as now I can hear him, beneath his breath, sing a little song whose only lyric is the word Dunes.

Still thinking about it, huh? I say.

He looks at me then, like he's never seen me before. Then his eyes dig through that brain fog of his, as we are walking, and he says of course he's still thinking about it. It's like Eden, he says, just like fucking Tigris and Euphrates, just like that Rousseau painting with the naked woman on the couch, and I have to tell him I never saw that picture before, so I don't know really what he means. He says forget it, just fucking forget it, and we walk on through the crowds.

Across the street from the grade school we pass a diner. Paul turns inside its door, tells me come on, we're ahead of schedule, he has to eat. He is all appetite, everything about him tries to be fed continually. He stands in the room's middle, looking out on professors and students who sip coffee, and laugh, talk about Marx and Hegel, Freud, and when I catch up, he looks at me a little wildly, looks back around the room and asks if I think they're laughing at him. No, I say, they're not laughing at you. A waitress comes up and says that way's smoking, if you want to sit there, and I say no, we want non-smoking. She points to a table that's got dirty dishes across but we can have, if we want. She says the bus boy will be by soon. She gives us a menu and so we sit.

You know, I say, we need to be in South Bend by noon.

Paul looks around the place till he finds a clock, which reads 8:20. Plenty of time, he says, then he loses himself inside the menu, no more than a cipher for now. He reaches out to take a half eaten roll from off a plate, bites it, frowns, and says they use margarine here, not real butter. He spits the roll into a napkin.

The bus boy takes away the dirty plates, the waitress finally comes. I decide on pancakes and coffee, but Paul insists to the waitress he wants pasticcio, even though it won't be ready for two hours. She rolls her eyes, says she'll see if there's any left from the day before. She snatches the menu from his hands and then leaves. Nice place, huh? he says to me, seeming to have forgotten the laughter. Yeah, I say, nice place. Paul's back is to them so he doesn't see the cops come inside and sit down at the counter, like I knew they would. Copper heaven, free doughnuts, free coffee any time. I knew better, way back when, than to walk 57th Street. I think that maybe I could've found a better traveling companion, sure, but no one else had money, and besides, Paul knows things, and sometimes some of what he knows is handy.

The waitress brings us each a cup of coffee. I put a drop of cream in mine, no sugar, but Paul, he quickly gulps some coffee, burning his mouth and lips, says shit, shit, but quietly, thank god, then pours cream in it, filling the cup past the top. He doesn't stir, but he drinks, a rivulet of cream racing for his chin. Man, he says, man. I needed that. The cream on Paul's face looks like a comma, and his mouth is open, so I wait for him to go on, but he stares into space instead, another molecule bubbling up, one thing more for him—and me—to contend with.

Paul, I say.

Uh, he says.

You with me? I ask.

Uh, says Paul, but he is making very little noise at this point, doesn't seem to be heading for one of his fits, so I put on a most serious face, edging it with tranquility, but in actuality I am scoping. A group of smart-ass collegy types sit beside us. Well dressed, expensive clothes. A Mediterranean, maybe Italian or Jewish, with his Waspy looking girl who sits beside him and talks in lock-jaw locution to some handsome preppy across from her. Just the three of them, looking to me like they probably fuck each other at the same time, or the girl fucks the prepster when the Italian isn't looking, or the prepster fucks the Italian, or wants to. Not so much older than me, or Paul. The girl sees me looking their way, but not the other two. She smiles at me and nods, so I smile back. It's one of those nice to meet you smiles she gives, but there's something dark beneath its niceness, something lurking, something fucked up, like you see every day walking the hallways of the hospital. Like I need this. I need to make my great escape into the world of civilization and find it lacking. But if I go back I don't see daylight, literally, for a year. And now in the real world Paul is sitting across from me and his eyes are rolling back into his head.

Hey, I say, but not too loud.

He says the same goddam thing: Uh.

I reach across the table, put my hand around his wrist, feel Lock-jaw watching me, squeeze it and Paul's eyes snap back. What? he says. Shh, I say, shh, and he sits very still and looks at me, then shifts his eyes quickly from side to side, taking in the room. He looks behind himself, sees the cops, and then looks back at me like some kid who might get whacked by his father, and I say don't worry, don't worry, they're just here for the coffee. I am using my most doctorly tone, having had recently so much experience with it, so much listening to it, and Paul nods and sits upright in his chair, just like he was anyone else. I pat his hand, and Lock-jaw sees it and grins lewdly to herself, thinking us two queers, but she's only half right.

The pancakes are good. I put a lot of fake butter on them, plenty of syrup, so much that the cakes are doing little backstrokes on my plate. The waitress even dug up for Paul his pasticcio, a block of what looks to me like macaroni, a meat-tomato sauce running through it, cheese baked on top, one big block that sits on his plate and he uses his fork to dig away at it, seeming to create, with each flaking forkful, some new arrangement, macaroni protruding in all directions. That's nice, I say to Paul, looking at his plate. He says it tastes good, but I can't have any, it's just for him. When we are done the waitress leaves the bill so Paul reaches into his pants and digs around; Lock-jaw the rich girl laughs, thinking, I guess, that Paul has chosen the here and now to play with himself, and I ignore her even though she is nudging the Italian to look at us. The handsome preppy turns to look just when Paul pulls a fifty out and slaps it on the table, shouting sold American. From the counter one cop turns to look our way, trying to pinpoint the shout.

Clouds have rolled up and the sky above the lake is completely gray when we exit the restaurant. We are walking the rest of the way to the train station, the sun still striking us but the clouds looking like they could dump snow along the rim of Lake Michigan, and the coffee has given Paul the shakes. His teeth are chattering some, even though it's not really cold enough for any serious shivering. You know, he says, as we're about to reach our destination, I got these memories. Caffeine dislodges them.

I know, I say.

I mean, my father used to do things, when I was little.

I know, I say, you told me before.

They were pretty awful, Paul says, and I tell him yeah, I know. I tell him all our fathers did things, and it was awful for everyone. We pass the park to our left, pass Dorchester, pass Blackstone, where, on the corner, sits another Greek restaurant. We pass by the used bookstore, cut across the street to where the station is, and there, standing right in the middle of 57th, Paul sees, through the underpass, beyond the bridge that carries the train, the museum his folks took him to once, when he was a kid. He starts jumping up and down and pointing. There are people around but it doesn't much matter. They're all minding their own business, this end of town more urban than the rest, a little more dangerous, a place not to walk at night.

Come on, Paul screams, and he starts running down the middle of the road in a straight line for the museum. I curse to myself, thinking if I had the money I'd just leave the sonofabitch. But I don't have money so I follow, running along the sidewalk hoping no car sprays Paul across the road. There's not much traffic here, not till we burst out from beneath the bridge into daylight and get to Stoney Island, where I catch up to him, catch him, grab him, shake him. I forgot it was here, he says, completely fucking forgot, can you believe it, that I forgot a place like this? He is looking at the museum, which is huge and covers acres of land, a lagoon and park to the south of it, a parking lot with ten thousand cars to the north, school busses sitting right in front.

South Bend, Indiana, I say to him, and he tells me this place is better than South Bend, and he begs me to walk with him out into the park, at least, if I won't go inside, just go to the park with him and sit awhile. I grab some jacket and pull him to the sidewalk, know we're going to miss the nine o'clock now and will have to wait for the ten, and so I start walking, Paul's piece of jacket in my hand, for the park. You won't regret this, he is muttering. Not at all, time of your life, you'll see.

There is a Japanese garden behind the museum that Paul insists we walk to, and we do, we walk along the frozen path, patches of snow lying in the shadows of trees. The garden has been terraced, and there is a footbridge that Paul walks up to, stands on, and smiles like a demon. This is where they put the body, he says.

Who? I say, trying to humor him, in my mind picturing the ten o'clock train rolling slowly toward us, hoping no one will look for us there.

Those two guys that killed the boy, Paul says. They put the body here, under this bridge.

What two guys? I say, and Paul's smile disappears while he strains to remember the names of who I don't know.

Begins with K, he says. Krebs and Kraul? But his face scrunches up, knowing, I guess, that Krebs and Kraul isn't right, not at all right. It bugs him he can't remember, and I know that once he was a smart guy, it didn't get any smarter, straight A report cards and all, so he starts to cry, Paul starts crying right there, standing in the middle of the Japanese garden out behind the museum, standing on the footbridge, crying because he can't remember the names of two guys who killed some kid. They were college students, he says, sobbing now. Two supermen, like Raskolnikov in Dostoyevsky. He's wailing now, like some gargoyle brought to life on those buildings back at the university, tears like rain running down the face of those big stone women whose heads hold up the roof at the museum. He obviously did not take his medication today, and I realize we hadn't even thought of that, thought what we would do once we got to South Bend. Paul's nutso, but me they got because I walked the streets, that's all. They figured me for a health hazard, and they didn't know what else to do but stick me away at the hospital. Back there the staff men would look at me, watch my ass when I walked down the hallways naked from the showers but then shake their heads, say to each other I could be carrying the plague. It's like that in the cities these days, you don't know who you can trust, who might give you what, who might whistle you into their cars and drag you, screaming, away.

Paul, I say. Paul!

His face is wet with tears, his mouth one big hole. So I shake him, pull him over to a bench, sit down with him. No one is around. It's too shitty a day for a Japanese garden, most coming here, probably, not till May, when the city thaws out from its awful winter.

He looks at me, finally, sees me. That's right, I say, it's me, Joe.

He nods his head, real fast. Yeah, he says, I know you're Joe, it's just I can't remember those guys, their names.

It's not important, I say, but he screams right into my face it is important, it's important to know stuff like that. He says he used to know more stuff than anyone, used to be able to watch *Jeopardy* and get every question, even the bonus round, even the daily double. His face has gone to shit as he's saying this, all red and his mouth is twisted and some foam is fuzzing up there at its corner. Okay, I say, so it's important, but what can you do, you know? What the hell, I figure, but Paul tells me it's the caffeine, he shouldn't've drunk so much goddam coffee back there at that Greek place. They got that special coffee, you know, he's saying, they all drink it, got that extra caffeine in it, and I say yeah, I know how they are, and he stops crying all at once and looks at me.

Don't patronize me, Joe, he says.

I smile, not knowing what else to do. I wouldn't shit you, I say, not knowing what else to say.

So Paul nods, thoughtfully, the water turned off completely. He sits up on the bench and tells me I should go get him a beer, tells me a beer will calm him down, tells me he wants me to go and get him a tall boy, some foreign import, maybe, and he's digging in his pants while he's saying this, pulling on his schwanz and he produces the other fifty and slaps it into my hand. I want a Foster's, he says. That big blue Lager number.

The guy at the liquor store remembers me, asks me where I been lately, and I tell him around, that's all, just around. He says some other guys disappeared, too, and I say so what and when I hand him the fifty he rubs his fingers along it and his eyes kind of glaze over. He says, You old enough to buy this?

Buddy, I say, I'm as old as the hills, which he doesn't get, since there aren't any hills in any direction for two hundred miles, unless they got some at the bottom of Lake Michigan, like those mountains that range up beneath the ocean. Paul read a story once where people lived down there, breathing water like it was air, sitting in chairs and reading their newspapers, some special ink, I guess, that doesn't run. He gives me forty-eight dollars and fifty cents in change, reaches beneath the counter for a paper bag that he slides around the Foster's, then twists it at the top like it was some bottle of liquor. Thanks, I say, and head for the door. Outside I tell myself that I have two twenties, a five, and three ones in my pocket, two quarters. Way more than a train ticket, enough to catch a bus south, once I get to South Bend. And no liabilities, going it alone, no one to fuck me up, to call attention to me on board some passenger vehicle, where everyone is just trying to follow the tales told in *Newsweek* as the print jiggles in front of them. At the end of the block, across from the park, just as I pass beyond the last building, the wind blasts me so hard that my arm flies out, and the fucking can of Foster's slips from my cold fingers and clunks down on the pavement. The bag is torn now, the can dented at the bottom.

In the park Paul is still seated on the bench. I know he will bitch when I hand him the Foster's and he does, saying I dropped the can, didn't I?

Yes, I say, I dropped the can.

He mutters something psychotic and unintelligible, and I say to him to just drink the shit and calm down. He pulls the tab open only slightly and beer foams out in a small geyser, and he looks at me not too annoyed and says Leopold and Loeb, it was Leopold and Loeb who killed the boy.

I heard of them, I say, and Paul says of course you have, they're famous. The beer stops foaming and Paul pulls the tab off and takes a long drink.

Isn't it cold? I say, and he's still drinking and his eyes, above the rim of the can, look at me like I am a lunatic. *Of course it's cold*, I think, knowing the things he thinks as he thinks them, *but it doesn't matter it's cold, I don't feel the cold, not like you, not with all the shit they pump into my system.* I sit down beside him and study the trees in this garden, small and twisted, gnarly, just like in the prints. They are beautiful, really, and Paul sees them, too, and studies them with me and seems, for the moment, to be at peace. But then he stares across the park, between the cypress trees in the direction of the museum, concentrating. Shit, he says, forgot that, too. What, I say. That, he says, pointing, and I focus my eyes in a line along his finger, ignore the trees and see it poised, on stone stilts, beside the museum. Even through the trees you can see its broken cross. They captured it out on Lake Michigan more than sixty years ago, he says. Now they use it for the tourists.

Motherfucker, I say, seeing it.

Yeah, Paul says. Motherfucker.

It mesmerizes him, the sub, and he studies it, not drinking for a while. Can't believe I forgot it, he says, shaking his head sorrily. Can't fucking believe it. We are quiet, some ancient thing inside us. *Everything means something, you have to know that, we are surrounded by things that aren't really themselves, ciphers, vessels, waiting for us to decide.* It tears him up to think about his home life. He wakes up nights screaming, saying he can still hear it, his sister's voice, and she's trying to tell me something but he can't remember the words. In one long drink Paul finishes the can of Foster's and, sitting, spirals the empty into a trash can. Now I'm okay, he says. Now I'm fine. He pulls a postcard and pen from his socks, telling me here, take it. The postcard is stamped and addressed to him, at the hospital. I hold it, confused, as he says, perfectly serious, This is as far as I go.

You're really not coming, I say, and he says no, he's not. Really. He tells me, not meaning, I think, to be literal, that he is just some angel whose job it was to see me to safe harbor.

I smile, then ask him why he isn't coming with me, and he says he can't come with me, he can't leave the city. Look on any map, he says, and you'll see a line that divides Illinois from Indiana.

Yeah? I say.

I can't cross that line, he says. Not anymore. It is a wall just as surely as the walls are walls back at the hospital. And this he means. He tells me to keep the change from the fifty. It's yours, he says. The twenties, the five, the ones and quarters. Yours.

So alone I ride the train for thirty-five minutes and get to the small town, a full hour west of South Bend, where the sign says Dunes. The lady on the train platform tells me it is a two mile walk through the snow, and jerks her thumb in the direction behind her. She is working a crossword puzzle and trying to think of a five-letter word for something. I think it's one letter more than I'm used to, and I walk off the platform behind her, start trudging through the foot of snow, lake effect, they call it, where the big winds come down from out of Canada, ride across the lake top and turn to snow when they hit land. Everything is white at midday, everything. Then they rise up in front of me, the dunes, big heaping piles of sand as tall as buildings, covered over on the south and east sides by snow, the wind having blown away the rest. They are all around me, the dunes, and at the top of one in the distance I see a chair, somebody's lawn chair from the summer. I walk to the west side of it, dig my shoes in, first one shoe then the other, making steps for myself as I ascend, hard work, but the wind is calm for once, it isn't here for me in Indiana, not today. At the very top, standing beside the chair, I look to the north and there it is and it's so big you can't believe, a rolling gray sheet. U-boat gray. I can hear it now as it crashes against the shoreline, beating it senseless. It pounds the sand into smaller pieces of sand, striking it till it doesn't know anything any more, it's not even sand at all now, just some pieces of nothing. I brush the snow from the chair, and take my seat.

In my mind I am writing on Paul's postcard, but I want to get it right before I put the pen to the rectangle. Dear Paul, I am thinking, and I know he is still sitting on that bench in the Japanese garden, admiring the cypress trees, trying not to look beyond them.

ABOUT THE AUTHOR

Michael W. Cox has published short fiction in such literary journals as *Cimarron Review, Columbia, Other Voices, Salt Hill,* and *ACM.* His stories have won a Northern Lights Fiction Prize from *Passages North* and been a finalist for the Flannery O'Connor Award, the Spokane Prize, and the Ohio State University Press Prize. His nonfiction has appeared in *River Teeth, New Letters, Kestrel,* the *New York Times Magazine,* and *Best American Essays.* He teaches creative and professional writing at the University of Pittsburgh at Johnstown.